# Murder in Vienna

## A LOTTIE SPRIGG MYSTERY BOOK 5

## MARTHA BOND

ISBN 978-1-7396766-7-4

marthabond.com

# Lottie Sprigg Travels Mystery Series

~

*Murder in Venice*
*Murder in Paris*
*Murder in Cairo*
*Murder in Monaco*
*Murder in Vienna*

# Murder in Vienna

## Chapter One

'I FANCY DOING a bit of shopping today, Lottie,' said Mrs Moore, giving her boiled egg a firm tap with a silver teaspoon. 'With regular breaks for strudel and hot chocolate. We could go to the Kar... Ker... oh, what's it called again?'

'Kärntner Strasse.'

'That's the one. Why is your German already so much better than mine? We've only been in Vienna for two days. Strasse means street, doesn't it?'

Lottie gave a nod.

'Strasse, strasse... if I repeat it enough, I'll remember it. I've forgotten all the other German words I'd learnt, though. It doesn't bode well for when I meet Prince Manfred, does it? Talking of which, hopefully I shall hear from him today. After all, he's the sole reason we travelled here.'

Lottie passed a piece of ham to her corgi, Rosie, beneath the table, and wondered if the courtship which her employer was longing for would finally blossom in Vienna. Keen to make the Bavarian prince her fourth husband, Mrs Moore had pursued him to Venice, Paris, Cairo and Monaco. Her persistence had resulted in a friendship with him, and the invitation to Vienna was a good sign. Since their arrival, however, there had been no word from him.

'I expect Prince Manfred is busy seeing his friends,' said Mrs Moore. 'He told me he has lots of friends here. Apparently, he was friendly with Charles I of Austria until the poor fellow was exiled to the island of Madeira and died there last year. I'm not sure why he was exiled. Perhaps his family wasn't popular with some people after his uncle's assassination started the war. Prince Manfred's interpreter, Boris, explained it all to me, but I find it complicated. I'm relieved Prince Manfred is from one of the minor European royal households. If you're from one of the important ones, then it seems you're at risk of assassination or exile these days. Awful isn't it? Oh look, a waiter is heading towards us with an envelope in his hand.' She picked up her lorgnette to see him more clearly. 'I can only assume it's a message from the prince!'

The waiter handed the envelope to her with a bow. Mrs Moore eagerly ripped it open, and Lottie watched her smile fade as she read the note inside.

'It's a telegram,' said Mrs Moore. 'Why would he send me a telegram?' Her face fell further still. 'Oh, it's not from the prince. It's from my sister, Lucinda! Oh, good golly.'

Mrs Moore's sister was Lady Buckley-Phipps. Lottie knew her well, having worked as a maid for her and her husband at their home, Fortescue Manor in Shropshire, England.

'What does it say?' asked Lottie.

'It's dreadful.'

'Is everyone alright?' Lottie felt concerned for the family and staff.

'I should never have sent my sister that letter about our plans to visit Vienna. Now our time here will be completely ruined!'

'Why?'

'Because Barty is arriving on the train at four o'clock this afternoon.'

'*Barty*? Here in Vienna?'

Bartholomew Buckley-Phipps was Mrs Moore's eldest nephew. After having worked at Fortescue Manor for five years, Lottie knew him as a lanky, likeable youth with a penchant for mischief.

'It says here he's been kicked out of Oxford,' said Mrs Moore.

'Oh no! Does the message give the reason?'

'No. But I should think his father is furious and I can only imagine Lucinda has sent him out here to get him out of his father's way.' She tossed the telegram to one side and sighed. 'I don't want to be responsible for Barty. I'm in Vienna to secure my fourth marriage! How can I do that with a feckless nephew in tow?'

'I can't imagine you'll have to look after him too much, Mrs Moore. He's twenty-one now.'

'Twenty-one and clueless. He clearly hasn't matured at all if he's been kicked out of university. I wonder what he did? Unfortunately, he's capable of just about anything. Why must I be burdened by him?'

'Lady Buckley-Phipps must be hoping you can help her during a difficult time.'

'I suppose so. But my brother-in-law, Ivan, has lots of brothers and sisters which Barty could be sent to. I can only imagine none of them are as far away as me. Lucinda and Ivan clearly want him well out of their sight. What a nerve they have sending him out here before even asking me!'

'Perhaps they knew you'd say no.'

'Yes, I should think that's the reason. Well, I suppose that's ruined our day of shopping.'

'We've still got time to visit the shops.'

'We'd be rushing about and having to keep an eye on the time because we need to be at the railway station for four o'clock. If there's one thing I hate, Lottie, it's being rushed.'

LOTTIE GLANCED around the impressive ticket hall of Vienna's South Station as they waited for Barty's train. A grand stone staircase stood at one end of the hall and the windows and lamps were ornately styled. Rosie excitedly tugged on her lead, keen to greet the travellers and porters passing by. Mrs Moore stood next to her, glum faced.

Lottie could understand why her employer felt despondent. She'd been given sudden responsibility for a wayward nephew and there'd still been no word from Prince Manfred.

The ticket hall began to fill up with people who'd just arrived on the four o'clock train. Lottie scanned the crowd for Barty's distinctive bouncing gait.

'I think I shall write to Lucinda and tell her I can keep an eye on him for only three days,' said Mrs Moore. 'That would be fair, I think. I feel I have to establish a limit. Otherwise, how long will I end up minding him for? It can't be indefinitely, that's for sure.'

They remained in the centre of the ticket hall as people around them embraced loved ones, chatted excitedly and issued instructions to porters wheeling their luggage. After a few minutes, the noise around them subsided.

'I might have known he'd keep us waiting,' said Mrs Moore. 'What's he doing?'

The ticket hall was almost quiet by the time Barty bounced towards them, a porter in tow. The young man wore a cream and beige striped suit with a matching waistcoat and a boater hat. Beneath the brow of his hat, his hair flopped into his bright blue eyes. He gave them a broad grin when he spotted them.

'Auntie Roberta! My favourite relative!' He pulled off his boater and held out his arms as he approached Mrs Moore. Before she could respond, he gave her a strong hug.

'And Lottie!' he said, still beaming after the embrace. 'Goodness, you look all grown up now. The last time I saw you, you were a young girl in a maid's uniform. How long ago was that? A few years?'

'It was Christmas when I last saw you, Barty. Six months ago.'

'Is that all? Well, doesn't time fly?'

Despite Barty's reputation for mischief, Lottie couldn't help liking him. She found his company entertaining and, at Fortescue Manor, he'd always been respectful to the servants. She suspected his rebellious streak was a response to his father's strict ways.

'Come along, Barty,' said Mrs Moore. 'Let's get you to the hotel.'

'Why are you looking so sour faced, Auntie Roberta? It's not like you.'

'Because you've been misbehaving again and you're here in Vienna as a punishment.'

'It's not a punishment if I'm here with my favourite auntie!'

'You can stop the flattery this minute, Barty, it won't work.'

'Oh it will, it always does. Can't we all cheer up a little? We don't want to have a thoroughly miserable time, do we?'

'No we don't.'

'And besides, there's been an enormous misunderstanding.'

'I can't imagine your parents have sent you here just because of a misunderstanding.'

'Oh, but they have! Please let me tell you my side of the story, Auntie. And once I've done that, then you may judge me however you see fit.'

'Very well. Now come on.'

'But not before I've said hello to this delightful little dog!' Barty bent down to pat Rosie. 'A Welsh Pembroke Corgi, if I'm not mistaken.'

'That's right,' said Lottie. 'Her name's Rosie, and we adopted her in Venice.'

'She's adorable,' said Barty. 'I'm so happy to be out of boring old Blighty. Now show me the hotel. I hope it's the best in Vienna!'

## Chapter Three

BACK AT THE HOTEL, Lottie and Mrs Moore had afternoon tea with Barty in the restaurant.

'What an assortment of cakes!' he said, his eyes wide at the sight of the cake stand in the centre of the table.

'They're quite wonderful, aren't they?' said Mrs Moore. Her mood was a little cheerier now. 'There's apple strudel, chocolate tart and many other cakes and desserts with long German names which I can't pronounce. They're extremely tasty, though.'

'That's what I like to hear. Now you take your favourite, Auntie.'

'Thank you, Barty.' Mrs Moore helped herself to a strudel.

'Now you, Lottie.'

'That's very kind of you, Barty.' She took a slice of chocolate tart.

'Not very kind,' he said. 'Because I plan to have the rest all to myself!' He laughed. 'I'm only joking, of course.' He took a slice of cake topped with cream. 'Now I can't imagine you were particularly happy when you received Mother's telegram this morning, Auntie.'

'It was a surprise.'

'More than a surprise, I'd say! You were no doubt annoyed at the thought of being burdened by my presence.'

'Not annoyed...'

'Ah, but you were, I can tell! I want to make it clear that I have every intention of not burdening you at all. I'm an independent man now and I can look after myself.'

'Is that what you were doing at Oxford? Being independent and looking after yourself? If you were, then I don't think you'd have been expelled.'

'Ah, but my dismissal was a misunderstanding, as I've already mentioned.' He licked cream off his fingers. 'I plan to go back there in September and talk the college dean round.'

'That will work, will it?'

'Of course! He's a thoroughly decent chap at heart. He was just a bit miffed with me, that's all.'

'So why were you expelled?'

'I went on a little punting trip on the River Cherwell with the college dean's daughter.'

'Oh dear. So you were asking for trouble.'

'Not at all, Auntie! There's nothing wrong with a punting trip. The trouble was, we got lost.'

'How?'

'I don't know how it happened, exactly. One moment we were happily punting along and then I realised we'd left the city behind and were somewhere out in the sticks. Then I lost the pole.'

'You lost it?'

'Yes! It got stuck in some duckweed and, in my attempt to free it, the pole slipped out of my hand and sank down into the depths. I wanted to jump in and fetch it, but Florence wouldn't hear of it.'

'Florence?'

'The dean's daughter. She got terribly worried about the

thought of me jumping in and said I might drown. So we were adrift! Floating to goodness knows where. Luckily we had a well-stocked picnic hamper with us. We got through the food and then night fell.'

'Oh dear. The dean must have been very worried about his daughter.'

'I dare say he was, but I looked after her. Eventually we were rescued by a ploughman at first light the following morning. He was on his way to plough a field. He took us back to Oxford in a trailer fixed to the back of his tractor. It was a bumpy ride! I've still got the bruises on my you-know-what.'

'Barty!'

'Sorry. Anyway, I lost money on the punt because I didn't manage to return it or the pole.'

'What a catastrophe, Barty.'

'It was! And the dean didn't take kindly to me keeping his daughter out all night and so he gave me the old heave-ho.'

'And what did your father say about it?'

'What *didn't* he say about it would be a better question. I don't believe I've ever heard such a torrent of anger and outrage! And to make matters worse, the Fatherly Figure refused to listen to my explanation! He was so angry, he was unable to stop shouting. In fact, no one believed me or Florence. It was dreadfully upsetting. So now Mother and Father think I'm a disgrace. That's why I've been sent away to my dear Auntie Roberta in Vienna and I've been told to stay here until everyone's calmed down. I don't know how long that's going to take. But at least I get to see you, Auntie, so there's a happy ending to the story after all, isn't there? And I should like to take this opportunity to make an announcement.'

'What announcement is that, Barty?'

'That I'm turning over a new leaf.'

'Are you?'

'Absolutely. There's no denying I've got myself into a few scrapes over the years. Not all of them were my fault, and many of them were misunderstandings, such as the punt and the dean's daughter. However, I think it's fair to say that mishap and misfortune have followed me around for long enough. My exile here in Vienna has already made me think about my actions and today, Mrs Moore, you see before you a changed gentleman.'

'Is that so? How lovely, Barty.'

'Thank you, Auntie. Already I'm quite different from the young man who left London yesterday.'

'I'm delighted to hear it.'

'And I'm quite sure that, before the week is out, you will see fit to put pen to paper and write to my father, telling him what a turnaround I have made.'

'In less than a week?'

'In less than a week. I shall prove myself to you, Auntie.'

# Chapter Four

At dinner that evening, Mrs Moore was handed another envelope.

'This had better not be notice that another wayward family member is joining me here,' she said, giving Barty a sharp glance.

'I've already told you, Auntie, I'm no longer wayward. I'm a reformed character.'

'Good.'

A smile then spread across Mrs Moore's face as she read the message in the envelope. 'Finally, I've heard from Prince Manfred!'

'What does he say?' asked Lottie, relieved for her employer.

'It's an invitation to dinner at the Schönbrunn Palace tomorrow! That sounds very grand. And you're invited too, Lottie! Isn't that nice?'

'Yes. It's very kind of the prince to invite me, too.'

'We're to get there for late afternoon when the prince will give us a tour before dinner.'

'What about me?' said Barty. 'Can I come?'

'I'm afraid your name's not on the invitation.'

'Why not?'

'Because the prince doesn't know you're here, does he? You arrived only this afternoon.'

Barty pushed out his lower lip. 'Who is this prince, anyway?'

'Prince Manfred of Bavaria. He's Europe's most eligible bachelor.'

'According to who?'

'Everyone.'

'I've never heard of him before.'

'Well, I happen to be on extremely good terms with him and I'm hoping he'll be my husband one day.'

'You want to get married again, Auntie?'

'Yes. Why not?'

'I thought you were tired of marriage?'

'I said that when I arrived in England after my third husband left me for that dancer from Petoskey. But that was before I heard about Prince Manfred.'

'You're actually going to marry a Bavarian prince, Auntie?'

'I hope to, yes.'

'What will you be then? Princess Roberta of Bavaria?'

'Yes! Oh, it sounds wonderful when you say it out loud!'

'It does sound quite impressive. Even better than Lord Buckley-Phipps, which is what I'll become one day. That's if my father doesn't disinherit me.'

'I'm sure he won't if you've turned over a new leaf, Barty.'

'Thank you, Auntie. Can I come to your wedding?'

'Of course!'

'You're so kind. Now what am I going to do tomorrow while you and Lottie are at the Schönbrunn Palace?'

'You shall have to entertain yourself, Barty. I'm sure you'll manage it, given that you're an independent young gentleman who's reformed his ways.'

'Thank you, Auntie, for having such confidence in me. I'm sure I'll be able to entertain myself in Vienna's fine bars and nightclubs.'

'No, that's not a good idea.'

'Why not?'

'Stay away from the bars and nightclubs.' She wagged a finger at him. 'You don't want to get into any more scrapes. I think you'll be much better off staying here at the hotel and reading a good book.'

Chapter Five

A SHINY MOTOR car arrived at the hotel the following day to take Mrs Moore, Lottie and Rosie to Schönbrunn Palace.

Mrs Moore had dressed for the occasion in a violet gown with a voluminous skirt. On her head, she wore a matching hat with a brim almost as wide as a parasol. 'It will shade me from the sun,' she explained to Lottie.

'As well as anyone else who stands next to you.'

'What a cheeky remark!'

Lottie had chosen a low-waisted, marigold orange sundress with a matching hat. She hoped it would be smart enough for the event and cool enough for the heat.

The chauffeur helped Mrs Moore into the car. It wasn't easy with her large outfit.

'I think it may be best if you remove your hat,' he said.

'I can't, it's pinned to my hair. It took me ages to pin it at a certain angle. If I remove it, I'll never be able to recreate the look.'

Eventually, Mrs Moore was seated in the back of the car, her head at an awkward angle so she could wear her hat. Lottie and Rosie squeezed in next to her.

The car pulled away and they drove along an attractive, wide boulevard which led to the outskirts of the city.

'I'm still despairing about dear Barty,' said Mrs Moore. 'The young man has no concept of the responsibility which weighs on his shoulders. To think he's the oldest of twelve children! He's heir to the estate which my sister and husband have worked so hard to restore to its former glory. I'm extremely worried he'll fritter it all away. Just like his ancestors did. If it hadn't been for the money my father made in railroads, Fortescue Manor wouldn't have been saved at all.'

'Perhaps Barty will mature into a respectable young gentleman,' said Lottie, trying to find something encouraging to say.

'I hope so. But he needs to get on with it because he's already twenty-one. His father had hoped Oxford would make a man of him, but there's no hope of that now he's been booted out.'

The car pulled up to a set of wide gates with tall, white columns on either side. Beyond the gates, the sun dazzled on an enormous cream and yellow palace.

'Good golly,' said Mrs Moore, peering at the palace through her lorgnette. 'I've seen some places in my time, but this one takes your breath away, doesn't it?'

The gates were opened for them and they drove across a vast quadrangle to the front of the palace. As the car slowed to a stop, a familiar slight figure in a blue suit descended a set of sweeping steps from the first floor of the palace.

'Boris!' said Mrs Moore. 'How lovely it is to see him again!'

The prince's interpreter seemed dwarfed by the palatial surroundings.

Lottie and the chauffeur managed to extricate Mrs Moore from the car without dislodging her hat.

'How delightful to see you, Mrs Moore.' Boris gave a deep bow. 'And you too, Miss Sprigg. And you too, Rosie.' Lottie couldn't help smiling as the interpreter bowed reverently to the dog. 'Prince Manfred is expecting you,' he added.

'How lovely,' said Mrs Moore.

They followed him through a colonnade beneath the staircase and entered the formal gardens which stretched as far as the eye could see. Ahead of them, the grounds rose gently to an arched structure on the horizon.

'Well I never,' said Mrs Moore, looking through her lorgnette again. 'This place is enormous. It reminds me of Versailles in Paris.'

'There is some similarity between the two places,' said Boris.

Lottie asked what the structure was on the horizon.

'That is the Gloriette,' said Boris. 'A large summer house. There are wonderful views from there. We shall take a closer look at it shortly.'

'We're going to walk there?' asked Mrs Moore, a note of trepidation in her voice.

'Not at all,' said Boris. 'Here comes our transport now.'

They followed his gaze to where an open-topped carriage pulled by two grey horses was making its way briskly towards them.

A passenger sat in the carriage wearing a royal blue velvet jacket, a golden sash and a three-cornered hat with a single, white ostrich plume in it. With his luxuriant dark curls, moustache and jolly smile, there was no mistaking Prince Manfred of Bavaria.

The carriage pulled up alongside them and Prince Manfred hopped out, removed his hat, and kissed Mrs Moore's hand.

'The prince is delighted to see you again,' said Boris.

'Please give him my thanks and tell him how enchanted I am to be invited here. Does this palace belong to the prince?'

'No, it belonged to the Habsburg family until Charles I

was exiled. It was their summer residence. It is now the property of the Austrian Republic, and Prince Manfred has rented it for a week.'

'Rented it? I can't even imagine how much that must cost.'

'I believe the term in English is *a pretty penny*.'

'That sounds about right.'

'Prince Manfred has rented the palace and some extra staff for his week's stay. He plans to entertain every night. It's going to be lots of fun!'

Prince Manfred's elaborate clothes impressed Lottie. He was dressed as if he were a Habsburg himself. He had a lace collar and cuffs and sparkling rings on his fingers. Even the buttons on his jacket had jewelled peacocks on them.


Soon, the four of them were seated in the carriage, and Rosie sat on Lottie's lap. The horses trotted on and the carriage passed between formal borders where thousands of colourful plants were arranged in patterns. Lottie could smell the scent of the blooms on the warm air. 'What a lot of gardeners must work here,' she said.

'I believe two hundred gardeners are employed here,' said Boris. 'The grounds cover four hundred acres. So I suppose that means each gardener has two acres each!' He chuckled.

They passed trickling fountains, neatly clipped hedges and countless marble statues. Prince Manfred grinned as he pointed to each feature. 'Sehr schön,' he said after each one. 'Very beautiful.'

'It's no coincidence that Schönbrunn Palace has the word for beautiful in its name,' said Boris.

'Is that so?' said Mrs Moore.

'Translated into English, it means *beautiful fountain*.'

'Even though it's a palace?'

'Yes. It has a fountain though. Several, in fact.'

'How old is this place?'

'There was a house here in the sixteenth century, then the Holy Roman Emperor Maximilian II established the place as a hunting ground. Everything you see here was built or altered during the seventeenth and eighteenth centuries. And a little bit in the nineteenth century too. You know how it is, a new ruler comes in and they want everything changed.'

The carriage paused by a large pool with a rocky wall behind it. On top of the wall stood a tall, white obelisk and a larger, balustraded wall formed a semi-circle around it. Water poured from a grotesque face in the rocky wall and into the pool.

'This is the obelisk fountain,' said Boris. 'One of the best-known features in these gardens.'

Prince Manfred pulled a face like the one on the fountain, then dissolved into laughter.

'It was constructed in the eighteenth century,' continued Boris. 'The rock resembles a grotto and those statues you see there are river gods. The obelisk stands on the backs of four turtles.'

'Turtles?' said Mrs Moore.

'The ancient Egyptians revered them. The obelisk is covered in Egyptian hieroglyphics which are merely decorative and quite meaningless. The golden sphere on the top of the obelisk symbolises the sun, and the eagle perched on top of it represents the ruler.'

'So there's meaning in this river god Egyptian turtle grotto fountain?'

'Yes.'

'You're so knowledgeable, Boris.'

'I don't know about that. I just happened to have learned a little about this fountain. It's ostentatious, but I quite like it.'

'Sehr schön,' said Prince Manfred. 'Very beautiful.'

Lottie wondered if the prince was feeling left out while everyone else spoke English around him.

Boris pointed out more features to them as they continued on their carriage ride. 'You'll also find a menagerie in these gardens,' he said.

'There are animals here too?' asked Mrs Moore.

'Yes. We won't have time today to visit them. But maybe another day. And here we have the Roman ruin, the Ruin of Carthage.'

'Goodness.'

The carriage pulled up alongside a large pool which was framed on three sides by an elaborate crumbling structure. Broken statues stood in alcoves, and sections of stone lay on the ground.

'Golly, it's quite something,' said Mrs Moore. 'How old is it?'

'A hundred and forty-five years old.'

'Really? The Romans were still around then?'

'Erm, no. Not at all. These are fake Roman ruins.'

'They purposefully built a fake ruin?'

'Yes. Rather odd, isn't it? But at the same time, rather exquisite.'

'Very exquisite!'

'The ruins are modelled on the temple of Vespasian and Titus, the remains of which still stand in Rome. But the reference for this structure was an eighteenth-century engraving of the temple.'

'You're so clever to know all this, Boris.'

'I merely repeat what I'm told, Mrs Moore. Note the magnificent arch which dominates the scene. It has some very ornate stonework, doesn't it? The statues in the pool are river gods.'

'More river gods.'

'A reference to the importance of the River Danube which flows through this wonderful city.'

Prince Manfred gave a sigh and made a point of looking at his watch.

'I think we just have time to show you the Gloriette on the hill and then we shall return to the palace,' said Boris.

# Chapter Six

AT THE PALACE, they climbed out of the carriage.

'Prince Manfred would like to invite you inside,' said Boris. 'Soon the other guests will be here.'

'There are other guests?'

'Yes. An author, a musician and a psychoanalyst.'

'Goodness, they sound interesting. I don't think I can match up to them.'

'But you're an American heiress, Mrs Moore!' said Boris.

'That was something I was born into. I did nothing to earn it.'

'All of us follow a different path in life. I know the guests will be delighted to meet you. There really is no need to be modest about your credentials.'

Lottie glanced around and couldn't see Rosie anywhere. Then she spotted her trotting off through the formal gardens.

'Rosie!' she called after her. But the dog pretended not to hear.

She turned to Mrs Moore. 'Sorry, I'll have to go after her. I'll join you in a moment.'

'Of course, Lottie. Hopefully, she won't go too far.'

Lottie ran through the formal gardens after her rapidly retreating dog. Although Rosie was usually well behaved, she could be prone to sudden adventures on her own.

Lottie felt reassured that Rosie couldn't stray too far because she was confined by the boundaries of the grounds. But four hundred acres was large enough to easily lose a dog in.

Rosie vanished between two tall hedges, and Lottie followed. Stepping between the hedges, she entered an area of the garden which was closely planted with rose bushes. Little pathways led off in different directions, and the flowers gave off a beautiful, heady scent.

There was no sign of the dog. 'Rosie!' called out Lottie. But there was no response.

Which route had Rosie taken? There were several possibilities. Lottie chose a path and went on her way, calling Rosie's name as she went.

The air was warm and still. There seemed to be no one else around.

Eventually, she left the rose garden and found herself by a neat, emerald green lawn. A palm house stood at the far end.

Lottie marched over to it, hoping she'd catch sight of the little brown and white dog before long. But there was no sign of her, and Lottie soon found herself at the palm house. She peered in through the windows but could see nothing but large, leafy fronds. The doors to the glasshouse were closed, so Lottie surmised her dog couldn't have ventured in there without someone opening the door for her. Turning away, she headed for a statue of a man on a horse.

Although she knew Rosie couldn't have got far, Lottie was growing increasingly worried about her. Was there a possibility she could slip through a gap in the hedge, escape the palace grounds, and never be seen again?

Her heart thudded as she marched along the pathways.

She felt angry at Rosie for running off. Then she felt worried about her. Then she felt angry at herself. Why had she turned her back on her dog for a short while and allowed her to slip away?

She walked back to the rose garden, wondering if Rosie had found some shade there to rest in. Then she heard a voice from the other side of the hedge.

'Hello?' she called out.

'Hallo?' came the reply. It was a man's voice. Then he spoke some words in German.

'I'm sorry, I don't understand,' said Lottie. 'Do you speak English?'

'Yes, I speak English.'

'Thank goodness! Have you seen my dog?'

'Yes. There is a dog here with me now.'

'A corgi?'

'Yes, I think so.'

'Oh, thank you! What a relief!' Lottie grinned with joy, then realised she appeared to be conducting a conversation with a hedge. 'Where are you?'

'Just on the other side.'

'How do I get there?'

'Don't worry. Stay where you are and I'll come to you.'

A moment later, a young man in green overalls appeared from around the corner of the hedge pushing a wheelbarrow. Rosie sat in it, her tongue lolling with happiness. The gardener had dark hair, dark eyes and scratches on his face.

'Oh thank you!' said Lottie, amused by the sight of Rosie in the wheelbarrow. She picked her up and cuddled her. 'I'm so sorry about this. Did she attack you?'

'Attack me? No! Why?'

'You have scratches on your face!'

'They're from a hawthorn hedge I was cutting earlier. Hawthorn has very long thorns. Stay away from it if you can.'

'I'll try to. Thank you so much for finding my dog. I was very worried about her.'

'It was no effort at all. She just walked up to me. What's her name?'

'Rosie.'

'That's a nice name. I'm Josef. I work as a gardener here.'

'And I'm Lottie. My employer is a guest of Prince Manfred's today.'

'Ah yes. He likes to rent the palace when he's in Vienna.'

'Have you met him?'

'No, but I've seen him around the place. He enjoys walking with his lady friends in the gardens.'

'Lady friends?'

'Yes. Friends who are ladies. And he has man friends too. But he doesn't walk arm-in-arm with them.'

'But he walks arm-in-arm with his lady friends in the gardens?'

'Yes. And I suppose he would do. Apparently, he's Europe's most eligible bachelor.'

'Yes, apparently he is.' Lottie decided not to elaborate on Mrs Moore's plans to marry him. Josef's mention of the lady friends concerned her a little. 'Well I should get back to the palace.'

'Of course. Enjoy your evening with the prince.'

'Thank you. I'll try to. And I'll make sure my dog doesn't run away again.'

'She was no problem. It was nice meeting you both.'

## Chapter Seven

INSIDE THE PALACE, a footman led Lottie and Rosie through a maze of opulent rooms and corridors. Eventually he reached a set of ornate double doors which he opened to reveal a vast room furnished in dazzling white and gold. Enormous frescoes on the ceiling depicted robed figures floating among clouds.

Mrs Moore, Prince Manfred and Boris stood by a long dining table in the centre of the room. Although the table was large by everyday standards, it looked tiny in its colossal surroundings. The table was covered in sparkling glassware and eight velvet covered chairs had been placed around it.

'You found Rosie!' said Mrs Moore, her voice echoing across the room. 'Had she gone far?'

'Not too far.' Lottie glanced around the room as she made her way towards the small group. 'What an amazing place,' she said.

'This is the Great Gallery,' said Boris. 'It's not usually used as a dining room, but the prince thought it would be fun to host the dinner in here.'

'Fun indeed!' said Mrs Moore. Then she turned to Lottie.

'I wonder when the other guests will arrive? I find it quite embarrassing to be the first at a—'

They were interrupted by the shout of the footman. 'Countess Maria von Friedensberg!'

A red-haired lady in a sapphire blue gown strode into the room. She wore a mink stole across her shoulders and strings of pearls around her neck.

'Manfred!' she enthused, heading directly for the prince. The pair embraced, and Lottie noticed Mrs Moore shift awkwardly from one foot to the other.

Prince Manfred and the countess then talked rapidly in German, each throwing their head back with laughter at regular intervals.

'Prince Manfred seems to know the countess very well,' muttered Mrs Moore. 'Perhaps she's a family member? A sister perhaps?'

Lottie examined their faces for signs of a family resemblance but couldn't see one.

'And it's a little rude of the prince to engage in such fervent conversation without properly introducing us first,' added Mrs Moore.

Boris stepped over, presumably noticing the expression of discontent on Mrs Moore's face.

'Are the prince and the countess related?' she asked him.

'No.'

'No? They're just friends then?'

'Indeed, yes. The prince has a lot of lady friends.'

'I see. And I suppose it helps when they can also speak German.'

'Yes. The prince finds it much easier to speak to his friends in German. Which is natural, of course, as it's his mother tongue. His only tongue, in fact. I tried teaching him English once, but he has a short attention span.'

Prince Manfred and the countess erupted into more loud laughter and Mrs Moore's lips thinned.

'I tried learning German,' she said to Boris. 'I began when we were in Paris and did a little more in Cairo. Less when we were in Monaco. It's the sort of thing you need to keep up with, isn't it?'

'Absolutely,' said Boris. 'You need to practise every day.'

'And the trouble is, I have no one to practise with. Apart from the prince, that is.'

'You can practise with me, Mrs Moore.'

'With you, Boris? Well, that's very kind of you. I don't see you every day, though.'

'No. But we see each other quite regularly and you can always use those moments to practise a little German with me.'

'Can I? Now let me think... I remembered a few phrases from the book I bought in Paris, *Colloquial German*. What were they again? Oh, it's terribly frustrating when these things leave your mind. Ich eisse Roberta Moore.'

'Heisse.'

'I'm sorry?'

'It's ich heisse.'

'Oh, that's right, I remember. Silly me. Ich heisse Roberta Moore. Guten Morgen.'

'Morgen means morning. As it's now evening, we would say *Abend*. Guten Abend.'

'Right. Guten... what was what it again?'

'Abend.'

'Of course. You just told me that. Oh Boris, this is hopeless. I don't think I'm any good at learning a foreign language.'

'Of course you are! All you need to do is practise.'

'But I did just practise, and it was hopeless.'

'You mustn't lose patience. I'm tempted to say you're almost as impatient as Prince Manfred.'

'Am I? Well, it's nice we have something in common.'

A waiter brought them glasses of champagne on a silver platter, then Prince Manfred presented the countess to Mrs Moore.

'It is a pleasure to meet you, Mrs Moore,' she said.

'You speak English as well?' said Mrs Moore.

'Yes. And French and Bohemian too.'

'Bohemian? Goodness. And as you're a countess, I'm guessing you're from a distinguished family?'

'Of course. Although that's not important to me.'

'I see.'

'I make my own living.'

'Do you?'

'Yes, I'm an extremely successful authoress.'

'Are you indeed? Have you written a lot of books?'

'Yes, too many to count.'

'And what sort of stories are they?'

'Romance. Love stories!'

'How delightful.' Lottie sensed Mrs Moore wasn't warming to the countess, but she was doing her best to be polite. 'Which of your languages do you write in?' she asked.

'German.'

'It's a shame I can't read your books.'

'Perhaps one day they will all be translated into English. Prince Manfred adores them.'

'Does he?'

'They're all he ever reads.'

'It must be nice to have such a loyal reader.'

'He tells me they warm his heart.'

'Doctor Felix Fischer and Mrs Catherine Fischer!' shouted the doorman.

A grey-haired man with a neat grey beard stepped into the room arm-in-arm with a pretty, dark-haired lady in a garnet-red silk dress.

Prince Manfred threw up his hands with glee, then chatted enthusiastically to his new guests.

'Dr Fischer is a renowned and respected psychoanalyst,' Boris explained to Mrs Moore.

'I've never met one of those before,' she said. 'It's quite a fashionable topic, isn't it?'

'Very fashionable,' said the countess.

'Do you know Dr Fischer and his wife?'

'No.'

'But you know of them?'

'Yes, everybody in Vienna has heard of Dr Fischer.'

'Mr Percival Smallwood!' shouted the doorman.

A thin, pale-faced man, dressed head-to-toe in black, entered the room. He wore thick-lensed spectacles and a lofty expression.

The prince gave out a cry of joy and dashed across the room to give the man an embrace.

'Well I never,' said Mrs Moore. 'Who's this gentleman the prince is so pleased to see?'

'He's a British composer,' said Boris. 'Prince Manfred is extremely fond of him. The friendship began last year after one of Mr Smallwood's compositions moved the prince to tears at the Salzburg Festival.'

'Goodness. Have you heard any of his work, Boris?'

'I have indeed.'

'Did it move you to tears?'

'I can't say that it did.'

'Oh. That's disappointing.'

'It takes quite a lot to move me to tears. Prince Manfred, however, is a more sensitive soul. Ah, hello Dr Fischer. Please meet Mrs Moore, an American heiress.'

The grey-haired gentleman gave a bow.

'So what does a psychoanalyst do, exactly?' asked Mrs Moore.

'He studies the mind,' said Dr Fischer.

'And how does he even begin to do that?'

'By examining human behaviour. Every man is the product of his behaviours. I examine his motivation, his impulses, his reactions, his desires, his fears. And many of these are locked away in the unconscious mind.'

'And do you, by any chance, hold the key to the unconscious mind?'

A grin spread across his face. 'I do indeed, Mrs Moore!'

'Well, it's quite worrying to think that all these things are happening in our unconscious minds without us knowing about them.'

'Ah, but you do know about them. Just not consciously.'

'And that's the worrying part.'

'There is nothing worrying about it at all, Mrs Moore. If you listen carefully enough, you will find your unconscious speaks to you.'

'Really? How does it do that?'

'Through dreams, Mrs Moore.'

'Dreams? But my dreams make no sense at all!'

'They do if you analyse them.'

'I don't believe my dreams can be analysed at all, Dr Fischer. For example, last night I dreamt I was swimming in a sea of onion soup, and I came across a little cat who somehow turned into a horse and we rode through a forest of sunflowers to a little hut where I dined on gooseberry pie with King George V. What does that mean?'

He bit his lip. 'I'm not sure.'

'I ate quite a bit of cheese before bedtime last night, could that be something to do with it?'

'It could be.'

'Perhaps the cat and the horse and the king represent each of my husbands? Now there's a thought. I'm not sure what the sea of soup or the forest of sunflowers represent... perhaps they're challenges which I must navigate my way through. I can feel myself warming to this idea now. And as for the gooseberry pie. Well, it was quite delicious. An object of desire, perhaps. My affection for Prince Manfred, maybe?'

The psychoanalyst looked baffled. 'You think Prince Manfred is represented in your dream by a gooseberry pie?'

'He must be. What else can it mean?'

'I don't know. I'm going to have to think about it.'


THEY WERE CALLED to dinner and Lottie sat at the end of the table next to Mrs Moore. The composer, Percival Small-wood, sat opposite.

'Mrs Moore, how delightful it is to make your acquaintance,' he said.

'And yours too, Mr Smallwood.'

'Call me Percy, please.'

'Oh very well, then. You can call me Roberta. I hear you're a gifted composer?'

'Indeed I am.'

'I'm very impressed. How do you even begin composing a song? I wouldn't know where to start.'

'I sit at my piano and wait for the muse.'

'Muse? What form does that come in, then?'

'It can be anything. A memory, a sensation. Even a smell.'

'You can write a song about a smell?'

'Have you ever caught the scent of an evening primrose at the end of a beautiful summer's day?'

'I have. But how do you turn that into a song?'

'The sense evokes an emotion from deep within me.'

'From your unconscious mind?'

'I suppose it could be from there, yes.'

'How marvellous! You should speak to Dr Fischer about that. I think he'd be thrilled to hear how you write songs with your unconscious mind. In fact, you could become a subject of study for him.'

'I can't say I wish to be studied.'

'Why not?'

'It would reduce me to an object. It would constrain me. I like to float freely in the sphere of my imagination.'

'Well, it's a shame you don't wish to be studied because I think the psychoanalyst would be particularly interested in your sphere.'

'I refuse to admit others into it.'

'I see.'

At the other end of the table, Countess von Friedensberg was talking loudly at the prince and the Fischers. When she paused for breath, the prince emitted a loud 'Bravo!'.

Two waiters placed bowls of soup on the table. One of the waiters was about to place a bowl in front of Dr Fischer, but he stopped and took a step back. The second waiter muttered something to him, but the first waiter stepped away and placed the bowl in front of Prince Manfred instead. He was a young man with light brown hair and freckles.

His actions struck Lottie as strange. Why hadn't he wanted to serve the psychoanalyst his soup?

*Chapter Eight*

Countess von Friedensberg's voice echoed around the room as everyone sipped their soup. Lottie wondered what she was talking about.

'Where do you live, Percy?' asked Mrs Moore.

'At the foot of a mountain in Wales.'

'How delightful!'

'I need the solitude.'

'Of course. As much as I adore London, it's a noisy place,' said Mrs Moore.

'Dreadful place.'

'I wouldn't call it dreadful.'

'Oh, it is. Despicable. The noise and the dirt and people everywhere!'

'I suppose that's what cities are like. But surely your work is performed in London's concert halls?'

'Yes, it is. Unfortunately, it means I must travel there for rehearsals and performances. When I do, I make my visits as short as possible. There is nowhere quite like Wales.'

'So I've heard. Will you be performing at all while you're here in Vienna?'

'Other than this evening, no.'

'You're performing this evening?'

'Yes. The prince has asked me to put on some entertainment for his guests.'

'Oh lovely! I can't wait to hear what you've got in store for us. Perhaps I'll be moved to tears like Prince Manfred?'

'Perhaps you shall.'

'How much practice do you need to put in before a performance?'

'I play for eight or nine hours a day.'

'Really? I'm surprised your fingers haven't fallen off.'

The composer glanced down at his hands, as if checking they were still intact.

'Does your hotel room have a piano in it for you to practise on?' asked Mrs Moore.

'Oh no. I don't think the other guests would appreciate that! Fortunately, I'm able to use a practice room at the Imperial Academy of Music and the Performing Arts. I know some of the teachers there.'

'Well, that is useful.'

'Hello,' said a voice behind Lottie and Mrs Moore. They turned to see Mrs Fischer standing behind them.

'I thought I would visit this end of the table between courses. It's rather noisy up there.' She gave the countess a pointed glance.

'Your English is excellent,' said Mrs Moore.

'I am English.'

'Oh? Well, that's a surprise.'

'Here, have my seat,' said the composer.

'You're most kind.' Mrs Fischer made herself comfortable opposite Mrs Moore and Lottie.

'How long have you lived in Vienna for?' Mrs Moore asked her.

'About twenty years. I've been married to Felix for eight of those.'

She looked about fifty, a similar age to Mrs Moore. Lottie guessed her husband was fifteen or twenty years older than her.

'And what's it like being married to a psychoanalyst?'

'It's interesting.'

'Good. Do you take an interest in his work?'

'None whatsoever.'

'So he doesn't psychoanalyse you then?'

'Oh, he tries to! And I tell him off.'

'That seems fair enough.'

'Oh, here comes the next course. I'd better get back to my seat and endure more of the countess's voice in my ear.'

'What's she been talking about?'

'Her books. Apparently they're so successful that all the bookshops in Austria keep running out of copies and her publisher can't print more quickly enough.'

'How wonderful to be so successful.'

The waiters placed little plates of salad in front of each diner. Lottie noticed the waiter who'd refused to serve Dr Fischer was still keeping his distance from him. Instead, his colleague served the psychoanalyst his salad. Dr Fischer noticed the reluctant waiter on this occasion and gave him a sharp look.

'Have you had enough time to interpret the dream I told you about earlier, Dr Fischer?' asked Mrs Moore.

'I'm afraid not. It's a little more complicated than you realise. You would need to attend my consulting rooms.'

'Then what?'

'We'd begin with a series of one-word prompts.'

'Such as what?'

'We shall try a few ideas now. But this isn't a proper psychoanalysis session, this is just for fun.'

'I like the sound of this.'

'Usually I would ask you to lie on a couch and I would put you under hypnosis.'

'I don't like the sound of that!'

'Hypnosis is nothing to worry about, Mrs Moore. It is merely a state between waking and sleep.'

'I'm quite familiar with that. I'm usually in a state of hypnosis until about eleven every morning.'

'Very well. Let us begin. Window.'

'Window?'

'You tell me a word you associate with window, Mrs Moore.'

'Right. Erm... do you mean the beautiful, tall windows we have in this room? Or an ordinary window?'

'It can be any window. It's important not to give the object much thought. The idea is you respond with the first word which comes into your head.'

'For window? Erm...'

'You shouldn't spend any time thinking about it, Mrs Moore.'

'I shouldn't?'

'No. Let's forget about the window for now and try a new word. Now it's important you don't spend time thinking about it. You merely respond with the first word you think of. Because that's your unconscious mind speaking.'

'Is it? Goodness. Alright then. Give me a new word.'

'Bride.'

'Oh golly. Really? I've been a bride three times.'

'Just one word in response to mine, please.'

'Sorry. Can we do another one?'

'Friend.'

'Lottie.'

It surprised Lottie to hear this. She felt her face flush warm, and she smiled.

'Blue.'

'Red.'

'Money.'

'Rich.'

'Lake.'

'Beautiful.'

'Carrot.'

'Carrot?'

'No need to repeat it. I'll try another one.'

'Peas.'

'I'm sorry?'

'That was in response to carrot.'

'Very well. Let me try another word. Voyage.'

'Journey. The journey of life, in fact. I view life as a journey, do you, Dr Fischer?'

'It is a common interpretation.'

'So what did my responses tell you about my unconscious mind?'

'They don't tell me anything because we didn't conduct the exercise under the usual conditions. It was just for fun, remember?'

'Oh. I was hoping you might be able to tell me something about myself.'

'I can tell you have a busy and energetic mind, Mrs Moore.'

'Do I? Is that a good thing?'

'Absolutely.'

Prince Manfred got to his feet and tapped his wine glass with his spoon. Then he made an announcement which Boris interpreted into English.

'The prince thanks you for joining him at this excellent dinner in these wondrous surroundings. He is delighted to be spending this evening with this intimate gathering of special friends. He also invites you to a recital in the music room after dinner at which the talented Mr Percival Smallwood will play some of his compositions on the piano which once belonged to the great Charles I, Emperor of Austria, Charles IV King of Hungary, Charles III King of Bohemia and Charles III King of Croatia. May he rest in peace.'

Everyone applauded.

'That piano's belonged to a lot of kings, hasn't it, Lottie?' said Mrs Moore.

'I think they were all the same person.'

'Really?'

'One King Charles and four different countries. Or territories.'

'Europe is a very confusing place. I don't know how anyone is supposed to make sense of it. And as for European royalty…. I suppose I'd better learn some more about it if I'm to marry into it one of these days.'

### Chapter Nine

ONCE DINNER HAD FINISHED, Boris gave everyone directions to the music room. 'The performance will begin in fifteen minutes,' he added.

Lottie took Rosie for a quick stroll in the palace grounds. She kept her attached to her lead in case she decided to run off again. The corgi had behaved impeccably during the dinner, and Lottie rewarded her with some pieces of food she'd wrapped into a napkin and put in her handbag.

The sun was lowering in the sky, casting a warm glow over the gardens. Lottie would have preferred to stay outside and enjoy the evening in the grounds. But she felt obliged to accompany her employer to Mr Smallwood's recital.

'Let's hope it doesn't go on for too long,' she said to Rosie as they headed back into the palace.

She tried to recall Boris's directions as she made her way to the music room. There was something rather lonely about the palace's enormous, empty rooms. Habsburg ancestors hung gloomy faced in paintings on the walls. Lottie felt they were watching her, wondering what she was doing here. It wasn't the usual place a girl from an orphanage would find herself in.

Rosie trotted after her as she made her way through decorative doorways. She reached a staircase and was just about to push open another door when she heard voices on the stairs above her. She paused for a moment, wondering who was speaking.

'Do you think you might, for just one moment, stop analysing everything?' said Mrs Fischer's voice.

'I was merely stating—' It sounded like her husband, Dr Fischer.

'Yes, I know what you were merely stating. But it's remarkably tiring after a while.'

'Why are we talking in English?'

'Because if any staff are walking by, they might overhear.'

'Perhaps they speak English?'

'They're servants. It's unlikely. Now back to the point I was making. You can talk about something straightforward, you know, such as what the weather's doing. That sort of thing.'

'But I couldn't care less what the weather is doing.'

'I realise that. But can't you think about other people for a change? Some people like to talk about simple things such as the weather because it's easy and everyone has something to say about it. When you're analysing everything and using long words, it makes the conversation difficult for some people.'

'Are you asking me to suppress my intelligence for the sake of people who aren't as clever as me?'

'No, I'm not asking you to suppress anything. I'm asking you to vary your topics of conversation. I think it would be nice to talk about something light and pleasant now and again. Rather than something so complicated.'

'It's a shame you have a fear of knowledge, Catherine.'

'I don't have a fear of knowledge. How ridiculous!'

'I blame your father.'

'It's nothing to do with my father.'

'You have three older brothers, and your father valued their education over yours.'

'There's no need to bring this up now, Felix.'

'From a young age, you were conditioned to believe your own education was unimportant. The result is you now feel ashamed about your level of education.'

'There is nothing to be ashamed about! I have a fulfilling life with lots of interests and good friends.'

'And these days you are in denial.'

'About what?'

'About your shame.'

'I don't have any shame!'

'Ah, but you do. Do you recall that dream you told me about when you were invited to a society wedding and turned up with no clothes on?'

'Felix! I don't want to have this conversation right now!'

'I asked you what emotion the dream stirred in you and you responded with the emotions of shame and embarrassment.'

'Everyone has had that dream, Felix. Not just me.'

'And everyone who has that dream is hiding their shame.'

'Felix. Please, just stop. I really have had enough. It's exhausting!'

*Chapter Ten*

THE MUSIC ROOM was furnished in red and gold. Seven gold chairs with red velvet seats were placed at one end of the room. At the other end stood a gold grand piano with ornamental lion's feet. Smiling cherubs were painted on its side and an enormous glittering chandelier hung above it.

Mrs Moore, Boris, Prince Manfred and Countess von Friedensberg were already seated. There was no sign yet of the Fischers or Percival Smallwood.

Lottie sat next to Mrs Moore and Rosie lay down on the plush rug. The two waiters who'd served them at dinner brought around silver platters with glasses of brandy on.

Percy entered the room and strode over to the piano. He turned to face his audience then frowned when he noticed two empty chairs.

'Who's missing?' he snapped.

The door opened and Dr Fischer and Mrs Fischer stepped in.

'You're late,' said Percy.

'I'm so sorry,' said Mrs Fischer. 'We got lost.'

'The performance is beginning now.' Percy watched the

Fischers take their seats then said, 'It is a great honour to perform for you at the special invitation of Prince Manfred of Bavaria. And to perform here in Vienna! The world-famous city of music!'

He removed his spectacles and put them in his jacket pocket. Then he took an audible breath through his nose, closed his eyes and gave a deep bow. After this, he turned and made his way to the piano. He lowered himself onto the seat, pausing briefly to flip his coat tails over the piano stool before fully seating himself. He took in another breath, flung his chin up, closed his eyes and held his hands over the keys. The preparation was so dramatic that Lottie struggled to suppress a giggle.

Eventually, the performance began, and Lottie watched with astonishment as Percy's fingers danced over the piano keys. A sweeping melody filled the room, and Percy rocked and swayed on the piano stool. His eyes were closed, and he held an expression of rapture on his face. Sometimes he slowed the melody to a stop, leaning over the keys. Then his fingers raced off again, and he leaned back. It was such an energetic performance that Lottie imagined it must be exhausting.

She heard some sniffing noises and turned to see Prince Manfred dabbing his eyes with his lace handkerchief. Eventually, the song ended and everyone began to applaud. But Percy solemnly held up a finger and instructed them to stop. Then he resumed the piece. His fingers danced and his head bowed and swayed. Lottie could understand why Prince Manfred was so moved by the music. However, Percy's manner spoilt her enjoyment of it. She would have preferred to listen without having to watch him dramatically fling himself about as he played.

When the song finally came to a close, everyone was permitted to applaud. Percy stood up and took a bow. Lottie glanced around the room and saw Prince Manfred's face was red and wet with tears.

Then Percy sat back in his seat and began again.

An elaborate carriage clock sat on an ornate mantelpiece and Lottie did her best not to look at it. However, as the performance wore on, she felt her eyes being drawn to the clock with increasing frequency. After forty-five minutes, Mrs Moore grew a little restless and kept adjusting her hat and the position of her feet.

There was little doubt the performance was magnificent, but as the clock showed an hour had passed, Lottie felt impatient to do something else. Fortunately the music had lulled Rosie to sleep and her head was resting on Lottie's foot.

Percy played on. From the corner of her eye, Lottie could see Mrs Moore's head nodding. Should she wake her? She felt sure her employer would be embarrassed to fall asleep so Lottie gave her a nudge and Mrs Moore came round with a loud gasp.

Percy hit a wrong note and shot them a fierce glance.

After a while, Mrs Moore's head began to nod again. Lottie didn't dare try to wake her this time in case she made another noise which would put Percy off. Instead she left her and hoped he wouldn't notice.

Lottie was woken by someone clapping their hands. Percy stood by his piano, bowing. Mrs Moore jolted awake and joined in with the applause. But the applause seemed a little thin. Lottie glanced around and saw most of the seats were empty.

'Goodness,' said Mrs Moore. 'Where have they gone?'

Prince Manfred was missing. As were Dr Fischer, Mrs Fischer and Countess von Friedensberg.

Percy pulled out his spectacles and put them on. 'Good Lord!' he exclaimed. 'The room's almost empty!'

Lottie realised the composer was so short-sighted he hadn't noticed his audience leaving.

Percy strode out of the room and Lottie looked at the clock. It was half past nine, and they'd been sitting in their seats for nearly two hours. She couldn't remember falling asleep.

'Oh dear,' said Mrs Moore. 'I don't think Percy's very happy some people have wandered off.'

'Some left the room and the rest of us fell asleep,' said Lottie.

'Whoops.'

The only other people in the room were Boris and the two waiters. The waiters were grinning, as if sharing a joke. Lottie wondered if they were amused by the lacklustre appreciation of Percy's performance.

'Where did Prince Manfred go?' Mrs Moore asked Boris.

'It's a lovely evening out there, it wouldn't surprise me if he's gone for a walk in the gardens.'

'I think Percy's quite offended.'

'He is. But his performance went on a bit, didn't it? Although Prince Manfred was moved by it, his short attention span means he gets restless. He must have decided to go out for an evening stroll before it gets dark.'

'And who can blame him? What about the others? Have they all gone with him?'

'I don't know. I saw the prince leave first and then he was followed by Mrs Fischer.'

'I see.'

'Dr Fischer left a few minutes later, presumably to catch up with his wife. Then the countess left. I think it makes sense for all of us to go outside now and get some evening air.'

. . .

THEY STEPPED out into the large, gravelled area in front of the palace. The sun had just set, and the sky was turning red.

Boris strode off to find the prince and Rosie skipped about, sniffing at the flowerbeds.

'It's nice to get some air, isn't it?' said Mrs Moore. 'And it's nice to have a little break from the other guests. They're not particularly easy to get along with are they? The psychoanalyst chap is very serious minded. And his wife is rather miserable too. The countess is a little more interesting although she talks a great deal. I don't think she has any interest in anyone else at all, does she Lottie? She's one of those people who talks at you. I may as well be a doorpost for all she cares. I wonder what Prince Manfred sees in her?'

'He likes her books.'

'I suppose that's it. But for someone who must have a wonderful imagination, I find her remarkably dull. And Percy's an odd one, isn't he? It's difficult to feel relaxed in his presence. I worry I might say something which offends him. He has a certain look about him doesn't he? Like he's sucking on a lemon. Oh dear, listen to me Lottie, I sound terribly ungrateful. Here we are at this beautiful palace on a wonderfully warm summer's evening, and all I can do is moan about our fellow guests. I shall stop myself this moment and remind myself to enjoy it. So few people find the opportunity to be a guest at a place like this.'

'It certainly is an opportunity,' said Lottie. 'When I was in the orphanage, I never dreamt I would find myself a guest at a Viennese palace.'

'You've come a long way, Lottie.' Mrs Moore smiled. 'And you deserve to be here. We didn't know each other very well when I first took you on as my travelling companion. But you've proven yourself to be a loyal, friendly, intelligent young woman whom I've enjoyed travelling with.'

'Have I?'

'Yes, of course. I wouldn't have chosen anyone else. Not even my sister.'

'Thank you, Mrs Moore.'

'You're like family to me now. And so is this delightful dog, here, Rosie. And if it wasn't for you, Lottie, we wouldn't have Rosie either. Do you remember how you took pity on her when she was orphaned in Venice, and you hid her and hoped I wouldn't notice?'

'Of course I remember.'

'I noticed immediately, but I didn't want to say anything. And I'm glad I didn't because I can't imagine life without Rosie now.'

'Me neither.'

'A lot has happened in just a few months, hasn't it? Oh.' She stopped. 'Did you hear that?'

Lottie couldn't hear anything other than faint birdsong. 'What was it?'

'I could have sworn it was a shout. One of the gardeners trying to get the attention of another, perhaps. How many gardeners did Boris say this place has?'

'Two hundred.'

'What a number. There it is again, it was definitely a shout. Why did he shout a second time? Let's go and be nosy, I'm sure the sound came from beyond the hedge over there.'

They went on their way and were just reaching the hedge when Percival Smallwood appeared from behind it. His eyes were wide behind his spectacle lenses, and he was out of breath.

'Good grief!' exclaimed Mrs Moore. 'Are you alright, Percy?'

'No, not at all!'

His clothes were wet and his hair in disarray.

'What's happened?'

'It's Dr Fischer! He's dead!'

'DR FISCHER DEAD?' said Mrs Moore. 'How? Where?'

'I've just found him in the Roman ruin,' replied Percy, still breathless. 'He was in the water! I tried to save him but then I noticed an injury to his head. He must have slipped and hit his head and drowned!'

'Goodness, how awful!'

'I'm on my way to the palace to get some staff to help.'

'Alright, we'll come with you. We'll need to telephone a doctor too.'

They turned and marched back towards the palace.

'I don't know where everyone else has gone,' said Percy. 'I was walking around the gardens looking for them and I saw movement up by the Roman ruin.'

'What sort of movement?' asked Mrs Moore.

'It's odd. Because I think I saw two people. But it turned out to be just him. My eyesight's not particularly good at distance.'

'But even so, are you sure you didn't see two people?'

'No, I couldn't have. Only Dr Fischer was there.'

'But it's very strange that Dr Fischer should slip over and

drown like that,' said Lottie. 'What caused him to slip and hit his head?'

'That's a good question,' said Mrs Moore. 'And then end up in the water, too. That sounds to me a little more than just pure bad luck.'

'What are you suggesting?' asked Percy.

'I think you may well have seen a second person,' said Lottie. 'It could have been someone who attacked him.'

'I agree,' said Mrs Moore. 'I won't bore you with the details, Percy, but Miss Sprigg and I have encountered a few suspicious deaths recently.'

'You think Dr Fischer's death is suspicious?'

'It could be. I think we need to make sure the staff telephone the police as well as the doctor.'

## Chapter Twelve

DETECTIVE INSPECTOR FRANZ BERGER had thick grey whiskers and wore a dark suit. He addressed everyone as they sat on plush chairs in a blue and white drawing room. A youthful, thin-faced man accompanied him.

'I shall speak to you in English, as not everyone here is Austrian. I like to think my English is quite good.' He gave a proud smile before assuming a serious expression again. 'Now, it is my duty to inform you that we have found Dr Fischer dead in a pond at the Roman ruin in the grounds of this palace this evening. His body has been examined by a doctor and we believe we are dealing with a case of murder. Who's that talking at the back?'

'Me,' said Boris. 'I have to translate for Prince Manfred. He doesn't understand English.'

'I see.' The detective folded his arms and waited while Boris finished his translation. 'Would it be better if I spoke in German?' he asked.

'No,' said Mrs Moore. 'I'm American.'

'I see.'

'How do you know it's murder?' asked Percy.

'Because the doctor was struck on the back of the head by something heavy,' replied the detective. 'My men are examining the area and have found a section of ornamental stone which we believe was used in the attack.'

'And then he was pushed into the water?' asked Mrs Fischer.

'Yes.'

'Oh, my poor husband!'

'I am very sorry for your loss, Mrs Fischer. It is an extremely sad case indeed. Although I never met him personally, I heard wonderful things said about the man. He was clearly an expert in his field and highly thought of. He will be missed by many.' Mrs Fischer gave a sob. 'Now it's important for us to establish when Dr Fischer was last seen alive,' the detective continued. 'Who here was the last person to see him alive?'

'Well, he was in the music room with all of us watching Mr Smallwood's recital,' said Mrs Moore. 'Then I fell asleep and woke up and realised they'd all left.'

'You fell asleep?' asked Percy.

'I'm afraid it was the effect of your beautiful music.'

'Did anyone see what time Dr Fischer left?' asked Detective Inspector Berger.

'I saw him leave,' said Boris.

'And when was that?'

'I don't know exactly, but it was after Prince Manfred and Mrs Fischer left. I know Prince Manfred left at about a quarter to nine.'

'So he missed the last forty-five minutes?' asked Percy.

'Then Mrs Fischer left about five minutes after that,' said Boris.

'Is that correct, Mrs Fischer?' asked the detective.

'I don't know what the time was, but I agree it was about five minutes after Prince Manfred,' she said through sobs.

'I think Dr Fischer must have left about five minutes after that, because he was probably keen to find out where Prince Manfred and his wife had got to,' said Boris.

'I see,' said the detective. 'So you think Prince Manfred left at a quarter to nine, Mrs Fischer left at ten to and Dr Fischer left at five to.' He turned to his companion. 'Make sure you write all this down, Schmidt.' Then he addressed Mrs Fischer, 'Where did you go, Mrs Fischer?'

'Out for a walk. It was so hot in the music room. The music was beautiful, and I felt awful leaving Percy's wonderful performance, but the air in there was quite stifling.'

'And did your husband find you?'

'No.'

'So the last time you saw him was when he was sitting in the music room?'

'Yes.' Her voice broke. 'And if I had known it would be the last time I saw him, then I never would have left!'

'Of course. Now Prince Manfred left before Mrs Fischer, is that right?'

'Yes,' replied Boris.

'Did Prince Manfred see Dr Fischer after he left this room?'

They waited while Boris put this question to Prince Manfred. 'No,' replied the prince.

'I see. Did anyone else leave this room?'

'Yes, we all did,' said Mrs Moore.

'Right then,' said the detective. 'So we have Prince Manfred leaving the room first, followed by Mrs Fischer, followed by Dr Fischer, followed by... who was next?'

'Me,' said Countess von Friedensberg, raising her hand.

'And where did you go?'

'For a walk, like everyone else.'

'I've never had quite so many people walk out of my

performances before!' said Percy. 'My feelings are hurt beyond belief!'

'Your performance was captivating, Percy,' said the countess. 'But the music room was very hot and stuffy. And I must admit I wanted to find out where everyone else had got to. I worried I might be missing out on something.'

'Did you see any of them when you went out for your walk, Countess?' asked Detective Inspector Berger.

'No. The grounds are so vast, we all missed each other.'

'And yet someone was able to find Dr Fischer and murder him.'

'Yes, I don't know how they did that.'

'So, who was next to leave the room?' asked the detective.

'That was me,' announced Percy.

'You, Mr Smallwood? But you were the one playing the piano.'

'I know. I finished my performance and when I put my spectacles on, I saw the room was practically empty. The ones who remained had been asleep. I've never performed for such an ungrateful audience! I left the music room to find them, but instead I found Dr Fischer dead in the Roman ruin.'

'And what time was that?'

'Not long after I left here. I finished my performance at about half past nine. I think I found him at about a quarter to ten.'

'And from what Boris tells us, we think Dr Fischer left this room at five to nine,' said the detective. 'So there is a period of fifty minutes during which Dr Fischer was murdered. I shall have to interview each of you in turn and try to discover the truth.'

'Are you suggesting one of us murdered Dr Fischer?' asked the countess.

'If you cannot account for your movements between five to nine and quarter to ten, then you are a suspect, I'm afraid.'

'How awfully unfair!'

'It is, if you're not the murderer. I shall have to work hard to eliminate each of you in turn.'

'But me, Miss Sprigg and Boris didn't leave the performance until Mr Smallwood had finished,' said Mrs Moore.

'Very well,' said the detective. 'Although I would still like to interview you because you may hold some useful information without realising it.'

'Of course, Detective Inspector, we're only too happy to help.'

'And I couldn't have done it either,' said Percy. 'Because I was performing.'

'But you found Dr Fischer's body, did you not?'

'Yes. So I couldn't have done it!'

'Perhaps you carried out the crime and claimed you found him?'

'What? No! I would never have done such a thing! If I'd murdered him, I wouldn't have run about the place trying to get help, would I?'

'I don't know, would you?'

'Are you actually accusing me of murder, Detective?'

'No, but I regard you as a suspect, Mr Smallwood.'

'What's the difference?'

'It means I suspect you could have done it. I also suspect the other people who were out in the gardens at the same time as Dr Fischer.'

'But it could have been someone else entirely!' protested Mrs Fischer. 'A madman who broke in!'

'It could have been one of the gardeners,' added Percy. 'Or any of the other workers at the palace.'

Prince Manfred suddenly jumped to his feet, startling everyone around him. 'No!' he shouted. 'I did nothing!'

Boris stood up next to him. 'I apologise for Prince Manfred's interruption,' he said. 'I've just explained to him what this conversation is about and he's most upset that anyone could suspect him of murdering his dear friend Dr Fischer.'

'I'm sure he is,' said Detective Inspector Berger. 'Please inform him that if he's done nothing wrong, then he has nothing to worry about. And please also inform him I shall interview him first.'

## Chapter Thirteen

AFTER PRINCE MANFRED'S INTERVIEW, Catherine Fischer joined Detective Inspector Berger and his pale companion. The room they were using for interviews was panelled with shiny walnut and gold. Tall mirrors and windows reflected the light from the large chandelier which hung in the centre of the room. It was dark outside now. The first night without her husband was just beginning. How could she bear it? The thought caused a wave of grief to wash over her and she let out a cry.

'Are you alright, Mrs Fischer?'

'No!'

'I'm most sorry to hear it.'

'I don't understand why you're interviewing me now. I've just been widowed!'

'I realise that.' He spoke in a calming voice. 'And I know it would be best to leave you to grieve in peace. But I'm sure you can appreciate I have a difficult job. I need to gather as much information as I can about your husband and then I can quickly find the culprit.'

'Very well.' She dabbed her face with her handkerchief. 'But I don't think you'll get much sense from me.'

Detective Inspector Franz Berger had searching grey eyes which suggested a keen, intelligent mind. He seemed the sort who would detect a lie quite easily, and this worried her.

'How long were you and Dr Fischer married?' he asked.

'How does that question help you find the culprit?'

'It gives me background information.'

'But how could it possibly help you catch my husband's killer?'

'I've been doing this job for a long time, Mrs Fischer, and I've learned that the answers in cases like this can come from unexpected places.'

'I still don't see the relevance of the question.'

'I am building up a picture, Mrs Fischer. I realise this is a distressing time for you, but I urge you to cooperate. It will be worth your while. The quicker you answer my questions, the quicker I can find the murderer.'

Catherine Fischer didn't want to be asked lots of questions, and she felt sure he suspected her. It was uncomfortable having the eyes of the detective and his assistant trained on her. She took in a breath and reminded herself to remain calm. That way, she could answer the questions as calmly as possible without raising their suspicions.

She gave a large sob followed by a dramatic sniff. 'Very well. We were married for eight years.'

'Happily married?'

'Of course! Why wouldn't we be?'

'Not all marriages are happy, Mrs Fischer.'

'But ours was!'

'Any children?'

'No, we both considered ourselves too old for children at the time of our marriage.'

'How old were you?'

She considered it an impertinent question. But refusal to answer would probably be considered suspicious. 'I was forty-two.' She said the number as quietly as possible. 'And Felix was sixty.'

'Did you want children?'

'No.' She gave him a sharp look and hoped it would prompt him to change the subject.

'You're English?'

'Yes, but I've lived in Austria for twenty years.'

'Why?'

'Why not?'

'You live here in Vienna?'

'Of course.'

'And how did your invitation to this evening's event come about?'

'Prince Manfred has long been an admirer of my husband's work and we socialise with him whenever he's in Vienna. We've also visited him at his castle in Bavaria.'

'So, you're good friends with Prince Manfred?'

'Yes. The prince was very fond of my husband. And the feeling was reciprocated.'

'And you last saw your husband when you were watching the performance by Mr Percival Smallwood. How was your husband then?'

'He was watching a piano recital, what more can I say? We weren't talking because we had to be quiet.'

'How was his mood before the performance?'

'Normal. He was his normal self. He wasn't upset about anything, if that's what you're asking. My husband didn't experience moods like the rest of us. I believe he spent his entire life in the same mood. Detached and always in a state of deep thought. It was practically impossible to have a conversation about anything ordinary with him.'

'Did that cause a problem in your marriage?'

'No!'

'Any recent disagreements between you?'

'Of course not.'

'Had he fallen out with anyone else?'

'Not that I know of. He was always bickering with other psychoanalysts about things. But he told me that was part of the profession. They all had different ideas about the role of the unconscious mind and all that sort of thing, and they could argue all day and night about it. But I don't think anybody got offended or emotionally upset about anything. It was all discussion in the name of science as I understand it. All perfectly normal, apparently. I don't think I could ever completely understand my husband's profession.'

'Even though you were married to him for eight years?'

'It was his job, and I left him to it. Just as the wife of a butcher doesn't show any interest in various cuts of meat. I had to stop him talking about his work at home, though.'

'That was a problem?'

She knew the detective was trying hard to find a fault in their relationship, but she was determined to pretend everything had been fine. 'No, it wasn't a problem. I merely had to remind him that, after a hard day's work, he was better off talking about something other than psychoanalysis.'

'What did he talk about instead?'

'Not a great deal. I had to make the conversation and I would talk about what our friends had been up to or what book I was reading or something one of the cats did. He would show a passing interest.'

The detective sat back in his chair. 'This must have caused difficulties in your marriage, Mrs Fischer.'

'Why are you obsessed with finding something wrong, Detective? It wasn't a problem at all. It was just the way our marriage was. My husband was a genius, but he had flaws too. Don't we all?'

'We do indeed. So, in summary, your marriage was happy?'

'Extremely happy. And if you think I murdered my husband because I was unhappy, then you're very much mistaken, Detective.'

## Chapter Fourteen

PERCIVAL SMALLWOOD SAT in the drawing room, waiting for an opportunity to speak to Prince Manfred. The prince was currently being talked at by Countess von Friedensberg. Boris chatted to the American heiress and her young assistant. And elsewhere in the palace, Mrs Fischer was with the detective. Percy wasn't looking forward to his turn being interviewed.

In the meantime, it was imperative he had a word with Prince Manfred. He was growing tired of waiting and decided the best course of action was to interrupt the red-haired countess mid-flow. The prince didn't seem interested in what she was saying.

He got to his feet and strode over to them. 'I would like a word please, Prince Manfred. Quite urgently.'

The countess stared at him, mouth agape. 'Do you mind?'

'I'm afraid I don't. I've waited long enough to speak to the prince, and I must do it now, please. Before I'm called in to talk to that detective.'

Prince Manfred asked the countess what was going on and

she translated for him. The prince then gave a nod, summoned Boris the interpreter, and headed for the door.

Relieved, Percy followed him.

'So rude!' he heard the countess mutter behind him.

They walked through a few rooms before reaching the billiard room, where three enormous painted scenes hung on the walls. Percy felt sure he'd never seen paintings so large before. The billiard table stood in the centre of the room and Prince Manfred began arranging the balls for a game.

'I think the prince would like to play three-cushion billiards,' said Boris.

'Even though his friend was murdered just a few hours ago?'

'I suppose it provides a distraction. Grief can work in unusual ways.'

'I don't want to play,' said Percy. 'I'd just like a quick word.'

The prince picked up a cue, examined its tip, then passed it to Percy.

'I don't think we have time for a game,' said Percy. 'The detective will want to speak to us shortly.' He glanced at Boris, who gave him a baffled shrug.

Prince Manfred bent down and lined up his cue with the white ball. He then powered it into the yellow ball and smiled as it then bounced off three cushions before hitting the red ball.

'Please.' Prince Manfred gestured for Percy to take his turn.

'I'm hopeless. I can't play billiards to save my life.'

'Please.'

Percy sighed, bent down and aimed his cue at the white ball.

'Gelb!' said Prince Manfred.

'You're supposed to cue the yellow ball,' said Boris.

'I told you I'm hopeless,' said Percy. He drove his cue into the yellow ball and it rolled down the table, completely missing the other two balls.

The prince tutted, seemingly annoyed by having to play an inadequate competitor.

Percy appealed to Boris. 'Look, all I want to do is speak to the prince about payment for my recital this evening.'

The lack of enthusiasm on the interpreter's face suggested this was an unwelcome topic.

'Is there a problem?' asked Percy.

'No, there's no problem. With me, anyway. I think it's important you're paid for your work. It's just that the prince can be... a little bit funny about money.'

'As is so often the way with rich people,' said Percy. 'In fact, they're usually rich because they're so reluctant to part with it. But I really could do with being paid. Things are very tight for me at the moment.'

'Very well, I shall broach the subject with the prince. What's your fee?'

'Five hundred Austrian krone.'

They both waited as the prince took another billiard shot, then Percy listened intently as Boris put the question of payment to him. He couldn't understand a word of what was being said, but Boris appeared to be doing his best to be persuasive.

Prince Manfred's face sank as the conversation went on, then eventually Boris turned to Percy and said, 'Prince Manfred thinks you are an extremely talented musician and very kind.'

'That's nice of him. Have you mentioned the five hundred krone?'

'Not yet.' Boris said some more words to the prince. He responded by resting his cue on the table and walking over to a stool at the side of the room. He slumped down onto it, muttering as he held his head in his hands.

'What's he saying?' asked Percy.

'This has been the worst evening of his life.'

'I can imagine it has. It's probably even worse for Mrs Fischer.'

The prince continued to mutter.

'He says he can't think about money when he's upset,' said Boris.

'No, I don't suppose it's easy to think about much at all when you're upset,' said Percy. 'But I don't have any money and I performed here this evening in good faith that I would be paid.'

The prince lifted his head, placed one hand on his heart, and held out his other hand to Percy. He gazed at him imploringly, then spoke while Boris translated.

'He says you bring such joy to the world. Your musicality is a special power and expresses the emotions which lie so deep within all of us. Your compositions convey feelings with a power that words can never hope to achieve. You will never know how much you stir the emotions of a prince. Just like a spoon stirs the pot.'

Percy struggled to believe such nonsense. This wasn't the first time a rich man had expected him to perform for free and he was tired of it. 'Please thank the prince for his flattering words,' he said to Boris. 'However, I'd be far more flattered if he could cough up the five hundred krone which I charge for a recital. I've had to pay for my travel here and there's my accommodation to pay too. The prince has clearly spent a substantial amount of money renting this palace for the week. Surely he can find the money to pay me for my performance?'

Boris nodded. 'Yes, I'm sure he can.'

'So why isn't he doing it?'

The prince began speaking again.

'He says he doesn't know how anyone can think about money when someone has just been murdered,' translated Boris.

'Well, that all depends on personal circumstances, doesn't it? If you have lots of money, then you don't have to think about it too much. But when you have very little money and are relying on being paid for a performance, then you think about money all the time. I can't perform for free, you know! I deserve to be paid for my work just as much as the waiters who serve the prince's food or the chauffeur who drives his car.'

'Yes.'

'Can you tell him what I just said, please?'

'I will. Although I don't think he's going to be very happy about it.'

Percy listened as Boris translated his words.

The prince then sighed, got up from his seat and walked over to Percy. To Percy's alarm, the prince then put his arm across his shoulders, pulled an enormous lace handkerchief out of his pocket and began sobbing into it.

'The prince is overcome with emotion,' said Boris.

'I can see that,' said Percy through gritted teeth. He was staying in the cheapest lodgings in Vienna, but he wouldn't be able to pay for the room until Prince Manfred paid him. The landlady was harassing him for money. 'I think he's using his grief as an excuse for not paying me.'

'Yes, he could be,' said Boris.

Percy felt his anger get the better of him. He pulled away from the prince, leaving him unsteady on his feet. 'Well, now I regret ever coming here this evening!'

Prince Manfred stopped sobbing, seemingly surprised by the anger.

'I regret coming here and I want nothing more to do with you, Prince Manfred!' said Percy. 'You're rude and ungrateful and have no loyalty to your friends whatsoever!' Then he turned to Boris. 'Tell him what I just said, please.'

'Must I? I think he probably got the gist of it, anyway.'

'Please tell him what I just said.'

Boris did so, and the prince seemed most perturbed. He held Percy's arm and rattled off some sentences.

'He's very disappointed to hear your opinion of him,' said Boris. 'And he begs for your understanding. He says he will pay you the money tomorrow.'

'Tomorrow?' Percy couldn't determine whether this was a promise or an attempt to be rid of him. 'So I shall come back here tomorrow?'

'Yes,' said Boris. Then he lowered his voice, as if not wanting the prince to hear. 'I apologise for his behaviour.'

'I'VE ALREADY EXPLAINED THIS, Detective. Why would I raise the alarm after finding Dr Fischer if I was the one who murdered him?'

Percy ran a hand through his hair and tried to calm himself. After his infuriating conversation with Prince Manfred, he was now being accused by Detective Inspector Berger of being a murderer. The walnut room wasn't helping his mood. Its brown hue made him think of over-brewed tea. 'If I had carried out the deed, then I would have left the palace as soon as possible and taken the first train back to England,' he continued.

'And if you had done so, then you would have been the obvious suspect,' said the detective.

'Yes. And I didn't.'

'But I could argue that you committed the crime, then acted as someone who had discovered Mr Fischer's body. By acting in that way, you could have been hoping no one would suspect you.'

'No. Not true!'

'I've learned that murderers are clever, Mr Smallwood.

After they have committed their crime, they can attempt to manipulate events in the hope someone else will be blamed. Running away after committing the murder is an obvious thing to do. Many murderers I've come across like to do the opposite of what is obvious.'

'Well, I don't think like that at all, Detective. Probably because I'm not a murderer.'

'Very well.' He consulted some notes in front of him. 'I think it's worth noting that nobody appears to have fled the scene after Dr Fischer's murder. It seems our culprit has chosen to hide in plain sight. By doing so, they're clearly confident of their ability to defend themselves and are probably hoping a less confident person will get the blame instead. What do you think?'

'I wouldn't know, Detective. You're the one who's experienced in these matters, not me. My world is music. And I certainly wasn't expecting to come across the corpse of an Austrian psychoanalyst in a fake Roman ruin during my visit to Vienna. It's quite absurd! And extremely distressing for me. I worry that my creativity may not recover from this.'

'How well did you know Dr Fischer?'

'Not well at all. This evening was the first evening I met him.'

'Had you heard of him before you met him?'

'Yes, Prince Manfred had mentioned him to me. Via his interpreter, of course.'

'And how long have you known Prince Manfred?'

'About a year. One of my compositions made him cry at the Salzburg Festival last year. This is the first time he has asked me to perform a private recital for him.'

'Did you notice anything unusual about Dr Fischer during the evening?'

'Yes.'

'What?'

'He was unusual. He was one of those extremely intelligent individuals who seemed to exist in a world of his own.'

'Other than his character, was there anything else which struck you as unusual about him or his wife?'

'No. I barely knew the man or his wife, so I wouldn't have known if anything was out of sorts or not.'

'Did you notice any disagreements between them? Or disagreements between Dr Fischer and the other guests?'

'No. But then I'm not a particularly observant person. As an artist, I'm afraid I'm rather caught up in my own thoughts. It may sound inconsiderate to say it, but I don't find myself very interested in the affairs of others. I'm rather above it all, I'm afraid. I'm more attuned to sensations. Some people say I have a sixth sense.'

'Which means what?'

'It means I sense things which others can't.'

'A skill which could come in useful when trying to solve a murder. What do you sense about this particular case?'

'I... well, you've put me on the spot now, Detective. I can't answer you immediately. But it's obvious that Dr Fischer angered someone, and they put an end to him.'

'Indeed. One doesn't necessarily need a sixth sense to reach that conclusion.'

'No. Although I did sense something when I found the poor doctor dead in the water.'

'Which was what?'

'A terrible evil. Although the evening was warm, I felt a dreadful cold and darkness descend upon me. I felt then that evil was close by.'

He stared at Detective Inspector Berger and hoped there'd be no more questions.

## Chapter Sixteen

Percival Smallwood entered the drawing room, his face glum. 'He wants to see you two next,' he said to Lottie and Mrs Moore. Then he flopped into a chair, his arms folded.

'How did it go, Percy?' asked Mrs Moore.

'I thought I did a good thing by pulling Dr Fischer out of the water and raising the alarm, but that detective fellow seems to think I'm the murderer! The next time I come across a body, I shall stay out of the way and leave it for someone else to deal with.'

'Hopefully there won't be a next time!'

'I'm sure there will be if all we have is that hopeless detective.'

Lottie, Mrs Moore and Rosie made their way to the walnut room where they found Detective Inspector Berger and his assistant sitting at a walnut desk. The detective gestured for them to sit opposite him.

'And you have brought your lovely dog with you.' He smiled at Rosie. 'What does she think of Vienna?'

'She likes it very much,' said Mrs Moore. 'Although she's rather upset about the tragic death of Dr Fischer.'

'Is she? She doesn't look very upset.'

'No, but I'm sure she feels it. Dogs are sensitive animals. They pick up on things.'

'I'm sure you're quite right there, Mrs Moore. And thank you for joining us. It has been established you were both in the music room at the time of Dr Fischer's death, so please be assured I don't consider either of you to be suspects in the case. However, I'd be grateful if you could share your observations of the evening with me.'

'We'd be delighted to, Detective,' said Mrs Moore. 'Where would you like to start?'

'First, let's begin with a little background. Prince Manfred invited you here, is that right?'

'That's right. My assistant, Miss Sprigg, and I have been travelling and we've got to know him well along the way, haven't we, Lottie? We met him in Venice.... actually, I almost met him in Venice. But I met him in Paris, Cairo and Monaco. And then he invited us to his little gathering here in Vienna. I was very flattered by the invitation, of course.'

'How long have you known Prince Manfred?'

'I've known of him for about two years. It's no secret he's Europe's most eligible bachelor.'

'Is he?'

'Yes. Why do you look so surprised, Detective?'

'No reason. Do continue.'

'I was keen to meet him for some time and soon learned he's a tricky man to pin down. But I managed it in the end, didn't I, Lottie? And I've known him reasonably well for about two months.'

'Had he ever mentioned Dr Fischer to you before you arrived in Vienna?'

'No.'

'So the first time you met Dr Fischer was this evening?'

'Yes.'

'I realise you didn't know the man well, but was there anything that struck you as unusual about him?'

'Something suspicious, you mean?'

'Anything which didn't seem right.'

'No, everything seemed quite normal.'

'Anything unusual about the evening in general? Any disagreements between guests?'

'I don't like to be rude about someone who's died, Detective, but I did notice that Dr Fischer was a little odd. In fact, he reminded me of my second husband.'

'So he did disagree with someone?'

'I don't know. Sometimes the conversation was in German, so perhaps there was a disagreement then which I didn't understand.'

Lottie cleared her throat, realising now was her chance to speak. 'It could be nothing,' she said. 'But I overheard a disagreement between him and his wife.'

'Really?' The detective's eyes were on her now. 'What happened?'

'I was walking to the music room when I heard them talking in a stairwell.'

'And what was the discussion about?'

'Mrs Fischer was asking her husband to stop analysing everything and have a normal conversation.'

'And what was his response?'

'He said he didn't like normal conversation.' Lottie explained exactly what she'd heard.

'How angry did they get?' asked Detective Inspector Berger. 'Did they raise their voices?'

'No, there was no shouting, if that's what you mean. From what I've learned about them both, I suspect it was the sort of disagreement they had regularly.'

'I suspect so too,' said Mrs Moore. 'I can't imagine it was the first time Mrs Fischer brought the topic up. I suppose it came about because she was embarrassed about his social skills. It had become quite apparent during the evening that he would only talk about his work. I think she probably just wanted him to behave like a normal person in a social setting. But if she wanted him to behave normally, then perhaps she shouldn't have married a psychoanalyst. The profession sounds very impressive when you mention it to family and friends and I suppose he probably made good money from it. But in reality, I can't imagine it was much fun at all being married to someone so caught up in his own mind. Probably quite lonely, I imagine.'

'Did she tell you she felt lonely, Mrs Moore?'

'No, I barely spoke with the woman. It's just an assumption I've made. I've been married three times, Detective, so I like to consider myself quite experienced in spotting an unhappy marriage.'

'You think the Fischers' marriage was unhappy?'

'It had to be, hadn't it? Can you imagine putting up with him? I'm sorry if that sounds a little disrespectful.'

'Interesting. What you're telling me doesn't quite tally with what Mrs Fischer told me. She said their marriage was happy.'

'She would say that, wouldn't she?' replied Mrs Moore. 'For two reasons. First, no one wants to admit to a complete stranger that their marriage is unhappy. And second, if she admitted to a detective that the marriage was unhappy, then immediately she has a motive for murdering her husband, doesn't she?'

'Do you think she was capable of murdering her husband?'

'I don't know her well enough to say. But she could well have done. Miss Sprigg overheard the disagreement, and perhaps everything escalated from there. This is mere conjecture, Detective, but you did ask me to share my observations, so that's what I'm doing.'

'They're very helpful observations, thank you, Mrs Moore. I'd like to ask you about Percival Smallwood because you encountered him shortly after he found the body. How did he seem?'

'He was out of breath and agitated. He was also dripping wet. He told us he was wet because he'd pulled Dr Fischer out of the water in the hope he could save him.'

'Did you believe him?'

'At the time I did, I couldn't see any reason to doubt him. But now that we know Dr Fischer was murdered... well, it's possible Percy could have done it.'

'So when you saw Mr Smallwood in an agitated state, do you think he looked like someone who could have just committed a murder?'

'Yes, it's possible. It's rather difficult to be sure because discovering a body is going to put someone in an agitated state as well. And I can't think why Mr Smallwood would have murdered Dr Fischer. I understand the two only met for the first time this evening.'

'That's what I've heard as well.'

'And if Mr Smallwood did murder Dr Fischer, then he managed it remarkably quickly. He left the music room and then supposedly discovered his body just ten minutes later. That's a short amount of time within which to find a man within the vast grounds of the palace and murder him and then raise the alarm. I suppose it's possible he happened upon him purely by accident and immediately murdered him.'

'But why murder him so swiftly?' said Lottie. 'If he came across him by accident, then why would he murder him within minutes? There would barely be enough time for a conversation between them.'

'That's an interesting thought, Lottie,' said Mrs Moore. 'Perhaps we could consider the two men arranged to meet there?'

'But why?' asked the detective.

'I don't know. I think Mr Smallwood had the opportunity to murder Dr Fischer, but I don't know what his motive would have been or how he would have carried out the act so swiftly.'

'It was still possible, though,' said the detective.

'Yes, it was possible.'

'In which case, he must remain a suspect.'

'I saw something odd during dinner,' said Lottie.

'What was that, then?' asked the detective.

Lottie told him about one of the waiters refusing to serve food to the psychoanalyst. 'Dr Fischer noticed it too,' she added. 'And he gave him a look which suggested he might have known him.'

'Were any words exchanged between them?'

'Not that I saw or heard.'

'It's possible you've noticed some expressions on people's faces and interpreted them as meaning something.'

'You could ask the waiter about it.'

'Do you know his name?'

'No. But he had light brown hair and freckles.'

The detective made a note. 'I'll ask one of my men to speak with him, but I can't imagine there would be much to gain from it.'

'Ah, but there could well be,' said Mrs Moore. 'I'd advise you to listen carefully to what Miss Sprigg tells you, Detective. She has a skill for solving cases like this.'

'Really?' He gave Lottie a curious glance, and she felt her cheeks redden with embarrassment. She wished Mrs Moore hadn't mentioned it.

'Sometimes,' she mumbled. 'But I don't know about this case. It seems quite complicated.'

'You're right, Miss Sprigg,' said the detective. 'It's very complicated indeed. Thank you for your time, both of you. When you return to the drawing room, would you mind asking Countess von Friedensberg to join me?'

*Chapter Seventeen*

COUNTESS MARIA VON Friedensberg felt offended she'd been kept waiting for so long. When she was finally sitting in the walnut room, she pursed her lips and gave Detective Inspector Berger and his assistant sulky, hurt glances. Unfortunately, neither of them appeared to notice as the detective put his questions to her.

'When did you first meet Dr Fischer?'

'This evening. Or is it now yesterday evening? It's probably past midnight now because I've been kept waiting for so long.'

'That was the first time you met him?'

'Yes.' It was a lie, but she had to hope the detective believed her. 'But I knew of him, of course. Just like everyone else in Vienna.'

'Did you speak with him much during the evening?'

'Yes, he was very interested in hearing about my books. I wish we'd had the opportunity to speak longer because I would have been fascinated to hear all about his psycho-analysis work. But sadly it wasn't to be, and I feel sad I wasn't able to know him better before his untimely death.' She gave a sad smile and hoped it looked convincing.

'What made you leave the music room?'

'The same reason as everyone else. It was very warm in there and I was worried I'd fall asleep. The American woman, Mrs Moore, had already nodded off. Her assistant woke her up, which I think was the right thing to do. But she woke up so suddenly that she made a loud gasping noise. It put Percy off and he played a wrong note. I could see how annoyed he was about that, so I didn't dare risk falling asleep myself. So that was why I left. The other three had already gone by then.'

'Did you see any of them in the grounds?'

'No.'

'Where did you go?'

'To the rose garden. It's beautiful and smelt wonderful. Have you been there?'

'No.'

'Well, I quite lost myself in there and I had no idea anything was wrong until I returned to the palace and discovered poor Dr Fischer was dead.'

'Did anyone see you when you were walking in the gardens?'

'No, there was no one else about. I kept expecting to bump into one of the others. Prince Manfred maybe. Or maybe Dr Fischer and Mrs Fischer. But I didn't see any of them.'

'So no one can vouch for the fact you were walking in the gardens?'

'I'm afraid not, no. I wish now someone had seen me, because unfortunately I have no alibi for that time I was walking in the garden. All I can do, Detective, is to assure you I had no reason to murder Dr Fischer. I didn't even know him!'

'Did you notice anything suspicious while you were walking around the gardens?'

'Nothing at all. It was a beautiful evening. I watched the sunset, and that was quite delightful. I can't believe something so awful could happen on such a lovely evening. It doesn't seem right, does it? Poor Dr Fischer. I suppose the very best tribute I can make to him now is to have him as a character in one of my books. Do you think he would have liked that?'

'It's really not my place to say.'

*Chapter Eighteen*

'Hit over the head and thrown into a pond in some pretend Roman ruins,' commented Barty as he spread jam on his toast at breakfast. 'That sounds like jolly bad luck.'

'There's nothing jolly about it at all, Barty,' said Mrs Moore.

'No, I realise that. Just an expression.' He licked jam off his fingers. 'So did the doctor chap die from the blow to the head or drowning?'

'We don't know yet.'

'I suppose the blow could have knocked him unconscious and then the killer threw him into the pond, and he drowned because he couldn't save himself.'

'It's not a nice thought,' said Mrs Moore. 'And it's not something I wish to consider while I'm eating breakfast.' She cracked the shell of her boiled egg with her teaspoon.

'Bash,' said Barty, watching her. 'Just like the stone on the psychoanalyst's head.'

'Barty! That's enough! It's disrespectful and gory.'

Barty chuckled and chomped on a mouthful of toast.

'Anyway, Barty,' said Mrs Moore. 'What did you get up to yesterday while Lottie, Rosie and I were at the palace?'

'I went for a stroll around Vienna.'

'How lovely.'

'It's a pretty place, isn't it? And I found the houses where Beethoven and Mozart lived.'

'Did you really? How fascinating. I would like to see those places myself.'

'Then I came back to the hotel and went to bed early with a book of poems.'

'Did you? Gosh, you really have changed your ways, Barty. Your mother would be very proud.'

'I hope so. Perhaps you can write her a letter, Auntie, and tell her how well I'm doing?'

'In due course, Barty. You've not been here for twenty-four hours yet.'

'But surely you agree it's a good start?'

'Yes, it is. Keep it up.'

Barty took another mouthful of toast and gave Lottie a mischievous wink. She struggled to believe he'd gone to bed early with a book of poems. Was he really telling Mrs Moore the truth?

'Hopefully Detective Inspector Berger will make some progress today,' said Mrs Moore. 'He did a good job of speaking to everyone. I wonder what conclusions he's drawn. And as for poor Mrs Fischer... I can't imagine what she must be going through.'

A waiter approached the table and handed Mrs Moore an envelope.

'For me? Perhaps it's from Prince Manfred asking if we're alright. If it is, it's very kind of him to enquire. Poor Prince Manfred, his evening was quite ruined.'

She opened the envelope and pulled out the slip of paper inside. Lottie watched her eyes and mouth widen as she read it. Then she let out a cry and dropped the paper as if it were a hot potato. 'Oh good golly!'

'What is it, Mrs Moore?' Sensing bad news, Lottie jumped up from her seat and picked up the telegram from where it had landed among pieces of eggshell on her employer's plate. 'May I read it?'

Mrs Moore nodded but seemed incapable of speech.

The telegram was from Boris:

*Prince Manfred arrested for murder of Dr Fischer. On my way to you now.*

'Prince Manfred has been arrested for murder?' said Lottie, struggling to believe what she was reading. 'But he would never have done such a thing, would he? Dr Fischer was his friend!'

Mrs Moore nodded.

'Auntie, you look stricken,' said Barty. 'Would you like me to help you to your room?'

'Not yet. Boris has said he's on his way, so he will have an explanation for us, I'm sure. Let's wait in the lounge.'

A waiter approached, clearly concerned. 'Is everything alright?' he asked.

'Mrs Moore has had a bit of a shock,' said Lottie.

'She needs a medicinal drink,' said Barty. 'Have you any brandy?'

'Certainly, sir.'

'Please can you bring it to the lounge?' Lottie asked. 'I'm going to help my employer there.'


IN THE LOUNGE, Mrs Moore slumped across a velvet sofa.

'Oh, please tell me this is just a bad dream,' she said. 'Prince Manfred is the kindest, most generous gentleman I have ever had the fortune to meet. He always has such a spring in his step and he's so jolly! That's why everyone loves him. He hasn't a bad bone in his body.'

'A perfect gentleman, by any chance?' said Barty. 'Those are often the ones you have to watch out for.' Lottie shot him a glance to suggest he choose his words more carefully.

'How on earth can that horrible detective believe he murdered Dr Fischer?' continued Mrs Moore. 'I'll tell you what's happened. Someone has been telling tales. Someone has framed him. I think it must be the murderer. They've done something to make the detective suspect Prince Manfred, and he's fallen for it. And to think of poor Prince Manfred locked up in a police cell! It's truly awful. He'll never recover from it, he'll be so desperately upset!'

The waiter arrived with the brandy and Mrs Moore swiftly consumed it.

'Oh, what evidence can that detective possibly have?' she went on. 'None! I think he's swallowed someone else's lies. You put your trust in the police and then they make an appalling mistake. It shouldn't be allowed!'

'There, there, Auntie,' said Barty. 'I'm sure a proper explanation is forthcoming. The police don't arrest someone for no reason.'

'They do in Vienna! Oh, how could they? Is it because he's a prince?'

'The brandy doesn't appear to have worked,' Barty muttered to Lottie. 'Shall we ask for another?'

'Let's leave it a little longer. I'm sure she'll calm down in a moment. The news is still very recent.'

Barty agreed with a firm nod.

BORIS ARRIVED TEN MINUTES LATER. He wore the same blue suit as he always did, but his face was serious. Mrs Moore had calmed herself and cuddled Rosie on her lap.

'Oh Boris!' she cried out. 'Please tell me it's all been a terrible mistake?'

'Alas it isn't,' he said as he sat in a neighbouring chair.

'Barty Buckley-Phipps,' said Barty, holding out his hand to Boris. 'I'm Mrs Moore's nephew.'

'It's delightful to meet you,' said Boris, shaking his hand. 'I'm Prince Manfred's interpreter.'

'Jolly good. How's he bearing up?'

'Not good, I'm afraid.'

'Oh no!' wailed Mrs Moore. 'When was he arrested? Tell me what happened!'

'They came for him at seven this morning and the prince had to dress hurriedly. Detective Inspector Berger then told him he was arresting him on suspicion of the murder of Dr Fischer and then he handcuffed him.'

'No!'

'And took him away in a police van.'

'How awful! Where is he now?'

'At the main police station here in Vienna. It must be a mistake.'

'Of course it is! Prince Manfred has no reason whatsoever to harm his dear friend, Dr Fischer.'

'No, he wouldn't have harmed him.'

'On what grounds has he been arrested?'

'I suppose the detective seems to think he did it. Perhaps he has some evidence.'

'What evidence?'

'I don't know.' Boris shrugged.

'But what reason did the detective give? He must have one.'

'I have a vague idea what it could be.'

'So there *is* one?'

Lottie noticed Boris seemed reluctant to admit what it was.

85

'What is it?' asked Mrs Moore.

'Just something I'm aware of, but it's probably nothing.'

'You have to tell me!'

'Well, as I understand it, the two men had their differences.'

'What differences? I thought they were friends!'

'They were.'

'So what were the differences?'

Boris pulled a grimace. 'I think it's better that I don't say, Mrs Moore.'

'Nonsense. You will say!'

'I don't think it's something you wish to hear.'

'I wish to hear everything about Prince Manfred!'

'Everything?'

'Yes! I care deeply about him, and I want to know why he's been arrested.'

'And the reason you care so deeply, Mrs Moore, is the reason I don't wish to tell you.'

'Stop trying to protect my feelings, Boris. Whatever it is, I can handle it. I'm not a young delicate lady, I've dealt with many challenges in my fifty years. So you must come out with it.'

'Oh dear. You really insist?'

'Yes I do!'

Boris took in a breath. 'Very well. But don't get angry with me when I tell you.'

'Why should I be angry with you, Boris? You're Boris. No one can be angry with you.'

'Very well. I shall just come out with it.'

'Good.' Mrs Moore took in a breath too. 'I'm ready.'

Boris cleared his throat and Lottie watched him intently. 'The truth, Mrs Moore, is that Prince Manfred did have a motive for murdering Dr Fischer.'

'*What*?'

'Prince Manfred has been conducting a love affair with Dr Fischer's wife, Catherine Fischer.'

Silence fell. Silence which went on for so long that Lottie began to worry about Mrs Moore. Her employer sat motionless and staring into the air a few feet in front of her. She didn't appear to be breathing.

Boris didn't know what to do. He glanced at them each in turn, fiddled with his collar then adjusted the cuffs on his jacket. 'I'm sorry,' he eventually said. 'I really don't know what else to say.'

His words seemed to break Mrs Moore's trance.

She gave a slight nod, lifted Rosie from her lap, and placed her gently on the floor. Then she rose from the sofa and calmly walked out of the lounge.

## Chapter Nineteen

As soon as Mrs Moore had left the room, Barty turned on Boris. 'What's the meaning of this, sir? Can't you see how much you've upset my beloved auntie?'

'Yes, I'm so very sorry.'

'And so you should be!'

'Barty, this isn't Boris's fault,' said Lottie. 'He's just relaying a message. I agree that it's very distressing for Mrs Moore, but I don't think it could have been kept from her. She would have found out eventually and perhaps it's better she finds out now.'

'Well, I think it's darned upsetting!'

'I agree,' said Lottie. 'But please be kind to Boris about it.' She got up from her chair. 'I'll go and see how Mrs Moore is.'

She walked to her employer's hotel room with Rosie in tow and knocked cautiously at the door.

'Who is it?' came the weak response.

'It's me, Lottie. Are you alright?'

'No.'

'Can I get you anything?'

'No.'

'Shall I leave you in peace for a while?'

'Yes.'

'Alright then. I'll check on you again in half an hour.'

'Alright.'

Lottie turned to walk away. As she did so, she heard Mrs Moore calling her through the door. 'Lottie?'

'Yes?'

'Thank you.'


LOTTIE AND ROSIE returned to Barty and Boris in the lounge.

'How is she?' asked Barty.

'She doesn't want to talk at the moment.'

He slapped his thigh with annoyance and snorted through his nose. 'That dastardly prince... I've a mind to wring his neck!'

'I don't think Mrs Moore will ever speak to me again,' said Boris sadly.

'She will!' said Lottie. 'She knows this isn't your fault.'

'I should have told her sooner.'

'I think maybe you should have, yes. But presumably you feel a sense of loyalty to your employer.'

'Yes, I do.'

'How long has the affair been going on for?'

'About a year. No one is supposed to know about it because the prince didn't want his friend, Dr Fischer, finding out. But now Dr Fischer is dead, and the prince has been arrested, everyone will know. I wish I'd said something to Mrs Moore before now and then she wouldn't have wasted her time travelling here to Vienna.'

'But I don't understand,' said Lottie. 'If the prince was having an affair with Mrs Fischer, then why did he invite Mrs Moore on those excursions in Monaco?'

Boris shook his head. 'Prince Manfred was just being friendly. As Europe's most eligible bachelor, he receives a lot of attention from ladies and he enjoys it. He likes to encourage it, in fact. Although he was conducting a love affair with Mrs Fischer, it wasn't very serious because she was married and also he enjoyed travelling. They only spent time together when he was in Germany and Austria. He wrote her love letters while he was away. And while he was away, he liked to entertain ladies like your employer, Mrs Moore. It pains me to say it, but when we were in Monaco, there were other ladies he invited on excursions too. He couldn't help himself. The moment a lady showed him some attention, he encouraged it.'

It was clear now to Lottie that Prince Manfred had little thought for other people's feelings. 'He betrayed his friend, Dr Fischer,' she said.

'Yes, he did. I don't know what Dr Fischer would have thought if he had found out. Perhaps he did find out. And maybe that's why... oh, I don't like to think about it.'

'You think Dr Fischer's murder is a result of the affair?'

'I don't know. I can't believe Prince Manfred would be involved in such a dreadful incident. Perhaps it was an accident... I really don't know, Miss Sprigg.' His eyes were wide and desperate. 'I realise Mrs Moore is so awfully disappointed in him.'

'We all are!' said Barty. 'I don't even know the man, but Europe's most eligible bachelor? Who made that nonsense up?'

'He did,' said Boris.

Barty gave another snort and folded his arms.

'I should be on my way,' said Boris, getting to his feet. 'There is a lot to sort out with Prince Manfred's advisers and lawyers. He could be entirely blameless and be released again later today. But that does nothing to repair the damage which has been caused for poor Mrs Moore.'

'I think she'll be alright,' said Lottie.

'Do you think so?'

'Yes. She's got a strong spirit.'

Boris smiled. 'She certainly has. Please let her know I'm happy to assist her in any way I can. I've always been fond of her, and I like to think she will speak to me again after this.'

'I'm sure she will. She just needs some time to get accustomed to this news.'

'Of course. If you need me at all, you can contact me at the palace.'

'Thank you, Boris.'

Lottie and Barty watched him leave.

'Auntie should never have got involved with that dreadful prince fellow,' said Barty. 'He's nothing but trouble. Hopefully she'll realise now what a waste of space that man really is.'

'I'm going to take Rosie for a little walk outside,' said Lottie.

'Good idea. I'll stick around here in case Auntie needs something.'

*Chapter Twenty*

THE HOTEL WAS LOCATED close to Vienna's busy shopping streets. Lottie walked with Rosie along Kärntner Strasse until they reached the impressive Vienna State Opera house with its opulent arches and statues of horses on the elaborate roof. They turned right and reached a small park which was perfect for Rosie to run around and stretch her legs in.

As she watched her pet sniff at the manicured lawns and shrubs, Lottie felt her anger at Prince Manfred grow. It was infuriating that he'd encouraged Mrs Moore to believe she could have a relationship with him when he'd had no intention of marrying her. Boris had explained that the prince enjoyed the attention and Lottie realised now what a selfish man he was. There was little doubt that Mrs Moore was better off without him.

But despite his faults, it was difficult to believe Prince Manfred could be a murderer. He was obviously self-centred and thoughtless, but would he really murder someone?

There was little doubt Prince Manfred had a motive. If Dr Fischer had discovered the affair between Prince Manfred and his wife, then he could have threatened to tell people. Perhaps Prince Manfred had worried about his reputation and attacked the doctor to stop him from saying something.

Another theory Lottie could think of was the prince and Mrs Fischer had decided they wanted the doctor out of the way so they could marry. If that was the case, then Mrs Fischer could also be a murderer. Had the pair of them conspired to murder Dr Fischer?

Lottie recalled the conversation she'd overheard in the stairwell between Mrs Fischer and her husband. She'd seemed irritated by his poor social skills at the time, but it was clear now there'd been wider discontent in the marriage.

Prince Manfred had left the music room first, and Mrs Fischer had followed soon after. Had the pair arranged to meet somewhere in the grounds? Dr Fischer had followed them. Had he known they were conducting an affair? Had he planned to catch them together? If so, then perhaps they had both turned on him. Or perhaps they had both lain in wait for him and ambushed him.

Lottie shuddered. These thoughts were unpleasant, and she couldn't imagine the prince acting so cruelly. Was it possible that his jolly, fun-loving personality was just an act to hide an evil character?

BACK AT THE HOTEL, Lottie knocked tentatively at Mrs Moore's door.

'Come in,' said her employer.

Mrs Moore was sitting up in bed. Her face looked drawn and her expression was weary.

'How are you feeling?' Lottie asked.

'Angry.'

'I'm not surprised.'

'I've been taken for a fool.'

'You're not a fool, though.'

'I am! There I was, doing my best to acquaint myself with the prince and, all along, he was having an affair with his friend's wife.'

'But you weren't to know.'

'I should have known! The signs would have been there, I just didn't choose to notice them.'

'I didn't notice them, either. He was very charming to you, Mrs Moore, and you assumed he was a nice person.'

'Do you remember what the dear departed Mrs de Vere said about him in Cairo? I can recall the conversation clearly because I was so offended by her words. "I've heard the prince is little more than an overgrown child." That's what she said, wasn't it?'

Lottie nodded.

'And she went on to say that Prince Manfred had been spoiled since the day he was born and was incapable of tying his own shoelaces or combing his hair. Can you remember how angered I was by that, Lottie? I refused to believe it! And yet if I had, then I would never have allowed him to woo me in Monaco.'

'What Mrs de Vere said may not have been true.'

'There's no smoke without fire, Lottie. I think there must have been some truth in it. Why else would she say such a thing? I know she wasn't well liked, but she was straight talking. Oh, I've been so foolish, Lottie! I've wasted my time chasing after him. And I've wasted your time too!'

'You haven't, Mrs Moore.'

'I have!'

'No you haven't. I've enjoyed our travels.'

'Have you?'

'Yes. We've both met some fascinating people along the way.'

'I suppose we have.'

'And we've seen some wonderful places.'

'Yes we have.'

'We've been to places I never thought I would see. So none of it has been a waste of time for me. I can understand why you feel so heartbroken, though, Mrs Moore. He was mean to you.'

'He was, but... I'm not sure he did it intentionally. I was the one who pursued him, and perhaps he was just being polite. I don't suppose he was able to tell me about the affair because he presumably didn't want anyone else to know about it. But the fact he was conducting an affair with his friend's wife tells you everything you need to know about the man. He isn't Europe's most eligible bachelor at all. He's Europe's most dastardly scoundrel.'

Lottie couldn't resist a laugh.

'Oh dear, listen to me, Lottie. I could go on and on feeling sorry for myself, couldn't I?'

'It's understandable that you're upset.'

'Yes, it is. I have every right to be. But if I become a bore about it, you'll let me know, won't you? I don't want to become insufferable company.'

## *Chapter Twenty-One*

COUNTESS MARIE VON FRIEDENSBERG YAWNED, then plucked a grape from the fruit bowl on the table next to her chaise longue. She'd been kept up most of the night by the foolish detective who'd insisted on interviewing everyone immediately. And now he'd arrested Prince Manfred! There had been no need to detain the rest of them, after all.

Poor Prince Manfred. What evidence was there against him? Out of everyone at the palace, the prince seemed the least likely to brutally murder someone. And what could his motive have been? The detective had to be mistaken.

There was a knock at the door.

'Yes?'

Her housekeeper stepped in. 'Miss Kofler is here to see you, madam.'

'About time. Send her in.'

The countess consumed three more grapes while she waited. Moments later, a young woman entered the room carrying a heavy leather satchel. She had blonde bobbed hair and wore a fashionable baby blue woollen jacket and matching skirt.

'Anna!' said the countess. 'I was expecting you last week.'

'I realise that. I'm so sorry.'

'Never mind. Come and take a seat. No, not that one, it's for guests. Just pull over the stool from the window.'

Anna did so, then sat down and pulled a hefty manuscript out of her satchel.

'That looks a good size,' said the countess. 'How many words?'

'Seventy-three thousand, four hundred and fifty-eight.'

'You couldn't manage a nice round seventy-five thousand?'

'I thought about it, madam, but I really couldn't find an extra one thousand, five hundred and forty-two words. I worried they would end up being little more than boring waffle to fill the pages. I believe that once a story is told, then it's told.'

'I see. Well, I shall have a read of it and will tell you if it's missing something. Now tell me what happens in chapter one.'

'Young Lady Johanna is singing to herself in the summer house on a warm midsummer's evening. As she sings, she gazes at the pond where a dragonfly is swooping and diving over the lily pads. She has no idea that, close by, the gardener's son is secretly listening to her from behind the oak tree. The sound of her voice is so beautiful that a single tear runs down his cheek as he listens and he thinks of his dear departed mother.'

'A good start to the story. Now do the pair of them fall in love?'

'Of course.'

'But Lady Johanna's father disapproves because the gardener's son is of lowly birth?'

'Yes.'

'And who's the villain?'

'He's Count von Smeltzern zu Wildemannsek.'

'You'll have to change that name.'

'But why? I think he sounds perfectly evil.'

'Readers don't like long, unpronounceable names. It stops the flow of the story. Change it to von Cavallar.'

'I don't think it sounds as good.'

'Maybe not. But it's my name on the book cover, so I say it's von Cavallar.'

'Alright then.'

'So, I assume Lady Johanna is betrothed to von Cavallar, but the young gardener's son... what's his name?'

'Elias.'

'I don't like that. We'll call him Tobias. But young Tobias proves himself worthy of Lady Johanna's love, sends von Cavallar off to the hills, and the young couple live happily ever after.'

'Yes.'

'Good. Exactly the same plot as all my other stories. It sounds like you've done a good job once again, although I shall have to read it, of course. Thank you very much Anna. Once I'm happy with it, my secretary will put the cheque for fifty krone in the post.'

'Thank you, madam.'

'Just put the manuscript on the table over there.'

Anna got up from her seat and did so. She put the empty satchel over her shoulder but didn't immediately head for the door as the countess expected her to.

'Erm... it may be impertinent to ask this, madam,' said the young woman. 'But weren't you at Schönbrunn Palace last night when poor Dr Fischer was murdered there?'

The countess sighed. The murder was all Vienna seemed to be talking about. She wished she had never gone to the palace now.

'Yes I was. But don't ask me if I heard or saw anything

because I'm tired of that question. I had nothing to do with any of it.'

'It must have been very upsetting.'

'Yes, but more upsetting if I'd actually known the man. I barely knew him.'

'But he was well known.'

'I realise that. But he was also one of those psychoanalyst types and I can tell you now that they're the most boring people you could ever meet.'

'But I think it would be quite fascinating to talk to someone so knowledgeable on the topic!'

'I suppose some people might find it interesting. But the trouble with knowledgeable people is they can be such bores. Their entire lives revolve around one subject, and everyone must listen to them go on about it until they're bored to tears.' The countess then checked herself, worrying she might come across as unsympathetic. 'I don't mean to speak ill of the dead, however. Dr Fischer's death is a great tragedy indeed and his poor wife must be suffering terribly.' She pulled off another grape from the bunch.

'I heard she was having an affair with Prince Manfred of Bavaria.'

The countess paused with the grape halfway to her mouth. 'Nonsense!' she retorted. 'Where did you hear such a thing?'

'I heard it just now from a man I was speaking to in Café Mozart.'

'Really? It's unusual for men to gossip like women, Anna. I would pay it no heed at all.'

'How do you know it's not true?'

'Because....' The countess liked to think that Prince Manfred had eyes for only her. They'd had a wonderful time together in Dubrovnik just a few months previously. He'd also invited her to his Bavarian castle, but that invitation had been rescinded at the last minute. Was that because he'd been in love with Catherine Fischer? The miserable Englishwoman married to the old philandering psychoanalyst? She struggled to believe the prince would be interested in her.

'Just gossip,' she repeated.

'Oh, alright then.'

'But if it is true... Catherine Fischer must regret her infidelity now. It was a mistake of hers to take her husband for granted and now she's learned the hard way how awful it is when someone is taken so suddenly from you.'

'What a tragedy,' said Anna. 'I suppose the full details will emerge when Prince Manfred's trial is held.'

'Yes. That's if he did it. Some people are doubting it.'

'Do you think he did it?'

'I suppose he must have done.' She felt less sorry for the prince now she'd learned of his affair. In fact, she felt quite happy to pin the blame on him now. 'If the rumours are true, then maybe Prince Manfred conspired to be rid of Dr Fischer so he could marry his wife. Terribly brutal, but there you are. Although Europe's ruling families are mere shadows of their former selves, they still lead entitled lives and are prone to spoiled behaviour. It's saddening to learn that a friend of mine has done something so awful. How the mighty have fallen.'

*Chapter Twenty-Two*

'SO WHAT HAPPENS NOW?' asked Barty, helping himself to
an apple strudel.

'Now? This minute?' replied Mrs Moore. They sat in the
hotel restaurant enjoying afternoon tea. Lottie felt pleased to
see her employer eating and drinking, they were encouraging
signs of recovery.

'I mean the next few days,' said Barty. 'The reason you
came to Vienna, Auntie, was to see the scoundrel prince. But
now he's got locked up for murdering someone, there's no
reason for you to stay here any longer, is there?'

'Now you put it like that, Barty, I don't suppose there is.'
Mrs Moore cut off a piece of chocolate tart with her knife. 'I'd
envisioned seeing a little more of Vienna yet, but...' she looked
at Lottie. 'What do you think? Do we need to stay here?'

Lottie felt surprised and flattered for being asked. Usually
Mrs Moore was decisive about such things. 'I'd like to see
more of Vienna too,' she said. She also wanted to find out
who'd murdered Dr Fischer, but she chose not to mention it
for fear of reminding Mrs Moore about Prince Manfred.

'I suppose we could stay here for two more days,' said Mrs Moore. 'I want to see where Beethoven and Mozart lived.'

'They didn't live in the same house, Auntie.'

'Did they not?'

'No, different places.'

'Were they friends?'

'Now that's a good question. I don't know. Do you know, Lottie?'

'No. It's the sort of thing Boris would know. We could ask him.' Then Lottie winced, realising she'd reminded Mrs Moore of Prince Manfred.

'I don't think we need to see Boris again, do we?' said Barty.

'I like Boris,' said Mrs Moore. 'He must have found it very difficult telling me that news this morning. And perhaps I won't see him again. The thought leaves me feeling a little bit sad.' She took a sip of tea. 'Actually, I did quite a lot of thinking earlier.'

'Always a dangerous thing,' said Barty.

'It certainly is when you're concerned,' said Mrs Moore. 'But this turn of events has caused me to reflect on my behaviour. When I was chasing Prince Manfred across Europe and North Africa, what was I actually chasing? I don't think it was the prince. After all, I barely knew him! I'd only heard about him and I suppose I was drawn to the irresistible idea of marrying him and living in a fairy tale Bavarian castle on a mountaintop. But the likelihood of that happening was so slim, wasn't it? And if it had happened, then I think I would have got bored quite quickly. It may sound like a wonderful dream, but living in an isolated draughty castle in a country where I don't even speak the language... in reality, I think the novelty would have quickly worn off.

'And as for Prince Manfred, I don't feel I ever got to know him properly. I suppose the language difference had something to do with that. But even if I had spoken German, would I ever have got to know him? Was there even a personality to get to know? I wonder if he has no proper character at all. I wonder if he truly is that overgrown child which Mrs de Vere described so well.'

'It sounds like he is,' said Barty.

'I think I realise now what I was chasing,' continued Mrs Moore. 'It wasn't Prince Manfred. It was happiness.'

'You think so?' said Lottie.

'It's so common for us to get caught up in what we think happiness should be. We set ourselves targets and goals, telling ourselves that we'll be happy once we have them. But how often do we end up disappointed?'

'Often,' said Barty.

'Very often. And this heartache has made me realise that I need to look at my life as it is now and find the happiness here. Because it is here. Like you, Lottie, I've enjoyed the excitement of our travels. And I realise now that some of my happiest moments on this trip have not been with Prince Manfred but have, instead, been spent with you and Rosie and many of the entertaining people we've met along the way.'

'I'm happy you no longer view it as a waste of time.'

'I'm happy about it too. I've learned a lot about myself in just a day. Astonishing isn't it? I think I ought to be grateful to Prince Manfred for breaking my heart. It removed my foolish dreams and reminded me what's really important in life.'

For some reason, these words made Lottie feel emotional. She distracted herself by bending down to pat Rosie on the head.

'Hear, hear, Auntie!' said Barty. 'Let's raise a toast to that with our cups of tea!'

The three of them clinked their china cups together.

'Thank you, Barty,' said Mrs Moore. 'And a special thank you to you, Lottie. And Rosie too. There are some people -

and animals - who quietly get on with the business of being the important people in your life without any fuss.'

'Oh no,' said Barty.

'What is it?'

'Look who it is!'

They turned to see a small man in a blue suit making his way across the restaurant towards them.

Barty got to his feet. 'I'm going to—'

'You'll do nothing of the sort, Barty,' said Mrs Moore. 'Now sit down.'

'What does he want?'

'We'll find out.'

## Chapter Twenty-Three

'THIS IS A SURPRISE, BORIS,' said Mrs Moore. 'Do come and join us.'

Boris sat cautiously in a spare chair and Barty glared at him.

'How are you?' Mrs Moore asked the interpreter.

'I am well enough under the circumstances, Mrs Moore. How are you?'

'I'm absolutely fine.'

'Really? That is good news.'

'In fact, I've never felt better.'

'Oh. Even after the news that—'

'Yes, even after that news. In fact, it helped me realise what's really important.'

'I'm pleased to hear it.'

'It helped me realise that every moment is precious and is not to be spent chasing after a selfish overgrown child who has no cares for the feelings of others.'

'I see.'

'Even those he considers his friends! I refuse to feel sorry for myself any longer, Boris, but I feel so desperately sorry for

Dr Fischer. To think that a man he considered to be his friend was having an affair with his wife! What an awful betrayal for the man. I can only imagine his discovery of the affair precipitated his death.'

'I'm not so sure that's what happened.'

'Clearly it's what the detective thinks happened. And Detective Inspector Berger seems perfectly competent to me.'

Boris sighed. 'I've known Manfred for a very long time.'

'You poor fellow.'

'My father was his father's valet. We grew up together. It was a lonely existence for young Manfred in that mountaintop castle and he didn't have many playmates. We became friends.'

'If you're trying to make me feel sorry for him, Boris, you won't succeed, I'm afraid.'

'I'm just trying to explain how long I've known him.'

'You don't have to remain loyal to him just because you've known him since boyhood. Is it true that he has help to tie his shoelaces and comb his hair?'

'He does have some help with that.'

'I knew it! And to think I didn't believe it when I was first told. Mrs de Vere was right all along.'

'He's capable of doing those things himself, but he also has people to do them for him. I'm fond of him, Mrs Moore, but I will admit to you he can be lazy. Everything has always been done for him. He's accustomed to it.'

'The more I learn about the man, the more I'm reassured he would not have been a good husband. How relieved I am to have escaped his spell!'

'I realise Manfred isn't perfect and I understand the reasons why. I also think he has behaved atrociously by having an affair with his friend's wife. I warned him it would all go wrong, and I've been proven right. However, I know he wouldn't have murdered Dr Fischer.'

'How do you know that?'

'He's incapable of it. He's never harmed a living thing in his entire life. I remember he once devoted an entire day to helping a fly with an injured wing.'

'Really? How did he do that?'

'He tried lots of things such as using little, tiny splints and fashioning a replacement wing out of the finest silk, but sadly, nothing worked. But he tried, and that's the important thing. And it's that kind, gentle nature of his which convinces me that he will have had nothing to do with Dr Fischer's murder. He's an overgrown child, as you so rightly say, Mrs Moore.'

'Mrs de Vere said it first, but I'm pleased we agree on it.'

'So this is why I'm here this afternoon asking for your help.'

'*Help*?'

'I know Prince Manfred didn't commit this crime. I've visited Detective Inspector Berger today and tried to persuade him that Prince Manfred can't possibly be responsible. He won't listen to me. I worry his mind is made up and I fear he's stopped investigating the case altogether.'

'Probably because he's got his man.'

'But he hasn't! Prince Manfred didn't do it.'

Mrs Moore gave an exasperated sigh. 'What do you want help with, Boris?'

'I want you to help me convince the police that Prince Manfred is innocent.'

Mrs Moore laughed. 'And why should I do that after the way he treated me? And Dr Fischer?'

Boris nodded. 'I can understand why you feel that way, Mrs Moore. I find myself in a difficult position. I'm not proud of the way my old friend has behaved, but I also can't bear the thought of seeing him blamed for something he didn't do. And I also can't forget what a remarkable young sleuth this lady is.' He turned to Lottie. 'Miss Sprigg, I saw what you achieved in those investigations in Cairo and Monaco, and I was extremely impressed.'

'And Venice and Paris,' said Mrs Moore.

'As well? Then Miss Sprigg is truly a clever young lady. I'm wondering if you, Miss Sprigg, could put your mind to this case and prove to the detective that Prince Manfred isn't a murderer?'

Mrs Moore laughed. 'Miss Sprigg has better things to do with her time.'

Boris's expression was doleful. It was difficult not to feel sorry for him. He seemed to sincerely believe that Prince Manfred was incapable of murder. Was he right? Or was he fooled by him, just as Mrs Moore had been?

Lottie felt little inclination to help the prince. She felt angry with him after seeing how upset Mrs Moore had been. And although Mrs Moore claimed she was recovered, Lottie knew she was good at putting on a brave face. 'I don't know,' she said.

'I see,' said Boris. 'I understand why neither of you think the prince is worth helping. He's got himself embroiled in this mess, so he will have to find a way of getting out of it. I know you don't want to do it for him. But would you, at least, consider doing it for *me*?'

Lottie exchanged a glance with Mrs Moore and could see this was an appeal which her employer might struggle to turn down. Mrs Moore had always liked Boris, and it was clear he wanted to help his friend.

'I don't know either,' she replied. 'You're placing us in a difficult situation. I'm inclined to think that Detective Inspector Berger is very good at his job, unlike some police detectives we've encountered on our travels. That said, I can see how upset you are, and I don't think you deserve to be in this quandary. What do you think, Lottie?'

'I have little interest in helping Prince Manfred, but I

don't think it's right that someone innocent should take the blame for someone else's crime.'

'If it is someone else's crime,' said Mrs Moore. 'Let's not forget the prince may have done it.'

'I think he did it,' chipped in Barty.

'But Boris seems quite convinced he didn't,' said Lottie. 'And I'm inclined to believe him.'

'You are?' A slight smile flickered on Boris's face.

'There's no doubt you're quite sincere, Boris,' said Mrs Moore. 'And quite unlike your master in that respect. But I don't see why Lottie should spend her time trying to help that feckless prince. He has only himself to blame for his problems. And besides, Lottie and I have no reason to remain here in Vienna any longer. The entire purpose of our visit here was to spend time with the prince. He invited us here! And now it's all gone wrong. Why should we stay?'

Boris gave a sad nod. 'You're right. Why should you? The prince let you down and you have no reason to stay in Vienna a day longer. If I could pay you to stay, I would.'

'There's no need to pay us, Boris.'

'No. Very well.' He got to his feet. 'I tried, and that was the best I could do. If I don't see you before you leave Vienna, Mrs Moore, then I wish you the—'

'Oh wait, wait. I can't bear this!' said Mrs Moore. 'It's giving me a lump in my throat. You certainly know how to put on a sad face, Boris.' She turned to Lottie. 'Have you got any inclination whatsoever to give our friend Boris a hand?'

'Yes,' said Lottie. 'I would like to do what I can. If Detective Inspector Berger is mistaken about Prince Manfred, then we need to find out who the culprit is.'

Boris sank back down into his chair. 'Does this mean you'll help?'

'Yes,' said Lottie with a smile. 'We'll help.'

'*We?*' said Mrs Moore. 'I'm not sure I'll be much help. It will be largely down to you, Lottie.'

'I think we can all try to do something,' said Lottie. 'I may have had some luck in the past, but I can't promise I'll be able to find the murderer.'

'And there's a risk it turns out to be Prince Manfred after all,' said Mrs Moore. 'If, after all this Boris, we find out that it *was* him, I can't tell you how angry I shall be about it.'

'If that turns out to be the case, Mrs Moore, then you have every right to be as angry as possible. But thank you, both. You don't know how grateful I am.'


BEFORE BORIS LEFT, he wrote down the names and addresses of the guests and drew a little map of their locations so Lottie and Mrs Moore could speak with them.

'Oh dear,' said Mrs Moore, after he'd gone. 'I believe I've only agreed to this because I feel so sorry for him.'

'It's a bad idea,' said Barty. 'You should just do some shopping instead and then travel to whichever place tickles your fancy next. Why should you help the prince and his strange little friend?'

Mrs Moore nodded. 'We don't have to do this, Lottie. In fact, I don't even know where you'd begin.'

'It won't be a simple task,' said Lottie. 'But I would like to try.'

'What will you do first?'

'I met a gardener at the palace called Josef when Rosie ran off yesterday evening. I think he's a good person to start with.'

# Chapter Twenty-Four

'I WOULD LIKE to speak to Josef,' Lottie explained to the guard at the gates of Schönbrunn Palace the following morning. He wore a dark blue uniform with gold braiding.

'Josef?'

'He's one of the gardeners.' She made a digging motion with an imaginary spade, then felt foolish as he continued to stare at her impassively. 'Garden,' she added.

'Garten? Josef?'

Lottie nodded enthusiastically.

The guard held up a finger, which suggested she should wait. Then he went into the gatehouse and returned with a colleague who wore the same uniform. Lottie felt uncomfortable as the two men had a conversation, which included some pointing at her. Then they pointed at Rosie and appeared to discuss her, too.

'Josef?' said the second guard to Lottie.

'Yes. He's a friend.' Having only met him once, Lottie knew she was stretching the truth.

'Freund?'

She nodded again, relieved that some German words seemed to be similar to English ones.

After more discussion, a small gate within the larger gate was opened for Lottie and Rosie to walk through. The second guard said something to her and tapped his watch, which suggested she didn't have long. She thanked him, skipped through the gate, and headed towards the palace.

The sun was high in the sky and heat rose from the ground as Lottie and Rosie crossed the vast, gravelled quadrangle. They headed for the colonnade ahead of them, which Lottie recalled they could walk through to reach the gardens.

'Now where?' she said to her dog once they were standing in the spot where Prince Manfred's carriage had met them for the tour. Rosie trotted off in the direction she'd taken when she'd run off two days' previously. Lottie kept up with her this time, and they headed for the rose garden.

'I hope you're taking me the right way,' she said to her dog. The thought of trying to find Josef in the four-hundred-acre grounds was daunting. The rose garden was the place she'd met Josef, so it made sense to try there first.

Once they reached the tall hedges, Rosie turned one way, then the other. Lottie soon felt disorientated.

'Are you just playing?' she asked her. 'Or do you actually have a plan?'

It seemed silly to allow a dog to be in control. She wondered if it would be better to put Rosie on the lead and take charge herself. She paused for a moment, considering this. But it was a mistake. Rosie disappeared behind a hedge and Lottie lost sight of her.

'Rosie!' she called out. The rose garden was like a maze.

She thought of the guards at the gate, and how one of them had tapped his watch. How long had he permitted her to be here for? Was she destined to spend all her time here looking for her dog?

'Hello!' came a shout from the other side of the hedge.

'Josef?'

'Yes. Have you lost your dog again?'

'She was with me a moment ago, but now I can't find her.'

'Don't worry, she's here with me.'

Lottie laughed. 'I'm so pleased she's found you. You're the person I came here to see.'

'Me? Really?'

'Yes.'

There was no immediate reply, but then Josef stepped out from behind a hedge on her left with his wheelbarrow. Once again, Rosie sat in the wheelbarrow with the gardener's tools.

'And now I can say a proper hello,' said Josef with a smile.

'Hello and thank you for finding Rosie again. You must get lost in this rose garden regularly.'

'I know my way around now. But when I first began working here, I got lost regularly. Anyway, you came here to see *me*?'

'Yes. I hope I'm not interrupting your work.'

'Don't worry, it's boring work clipping these hedges. An interruption is most welcome. How can I help?'

'I'm quite shocked by the murder of Dr Fischer and the arrest of Prince Manfred. I'm trying to understand what happened that evening. Have you heard anything more about it?'

'People haven't stopped talking about it here. Everyone's very surprised Prince Manfred did it.'

'They're sure he did it?'

'Yes, a button from his jacket was found at the scene of the crime.'

Lottie gasped. 'So that's why he was arrested! Could the police be sure the button belonged to him?'

'Yes, apparently it was distinctive. It was silver with a

jewelled peacock on it. It matched the other buttons on his jacket.'

Lottie recalled seeing the decorative buttons when the prince had taken them on the tour of the palace grounds.

'That's quite strong evidence,' she said, wondering what Boris would make of it. 'Although it doesn't necessarily mean the prince lost his button there when Dr Fischer was murdered. He could have visited the Roman ruin before then.'

'It's possible.'

Lottie thought back to the carriage ride and felt sure she would have noticed if one of the buttons had been missing from the prince's jacket. 'But if he did visit the Roman ruin,' she said. 'When did he go there? And did anyone see him there?'

Josef shrugged. 'No one I know saw him there. And what made the button fall off his jacket? He could have caught it on something, but I think it's more likely it came off during a fight.'

'A fight with Dr Fischer?'

'It's the most likely explanation, isn't it?'

'Yes, it is.' Lottie sighed. 'I don't know what to think. Prince Manfred's interpreter, Boris, is an old friend of his and is convinced he's innocent. Boris has asked me to help prove the prince didn't do it. I don't think it's going to be easy.'

'Why has he asked for your help?'

'I've solved a few mysteries before.'

'Have you?' His eyebrows raised. 'Such as what?'

Lottie told him about her adventures in Venice, Paris, Cairo and Monaco. By the time she'd finished, Josef's eyes were wide with interest.

'I would say you're more qualified than Detective Inspector Berger to solve this!'

'No, I don't think so. I just agreed to help Boris. But now

you've told me about the evidence against Prince Manfred, I think Boris might have to accept his employer is guilty.'

Josef shrugged. 'It looks like it. But if an old friend is convinced he's innocent, then I suppose he should be listened to.'

'Did any of your colleagues see or hear anything that evening?'

'Yes, one of the waiters, Anton, was walking through the gardens on his way home when he heard raised voices.'

'What time?'

'Between half past nine and quarter to ten, apparently.'

'Male or female voices?'

'A man's voice,' said Josef. 'Although Anton was too far away to hear what was said.'

'Did the voice sound angry?'

'I don't know. I imagine so. Anton has told the detective about it, so hopefully it will help the investigation. I suppose the voice could have been Dr Fischer's, or it could have belonged to the murderer.'

'Or the voice may have had nothing to do with the murder.'

'It might not have done. It's unusual to hear something like that in a garden as peaceful as this, though.'

'And it fits with the timing of Dr Fischer's death,' said Lottie. 'Detective Inspector Berger says it must have occurred sometime between five to nine and quarter to ten. Dr Fischer left the music room at five to nine. How long do you think it would have taken him to reach the Roman ruin?'

'Ten minutes at least. And I've just remembered something else. A maid, Sonja, said she walked past the Roman ruin at quarter past nine and saw no one there.'

'So this could mean Dr Fischer was murdered between quarter past nine and quarter to ten.'

'Yes, I suppose it could.'

'Do you know if Anton or Sonja saw any of the guests as they walked through the gardens?' Lottie asked.

'I don't know. I suppose if they had, then they will have told the police about it.'

'I noticed something strange about one of the waiters that evening. He didn't want to serve Dr Fischer. How well do you know the waiters?'

'Not very well. They've been hired by Prince Manfred for the week, so they're not regular employees here. But we've all been talking a lot since Dr Fischer's death.'

'The waiter who didn't want to serve Dr Fischer had light brown hair and freckles.'

'That sounds like Anton to me.'

'The same Anton who heard a shout in the gardens?'

'Yes, I think it's him.'

'Do you think I could speak to him?'

'I'm not sure. I'll ask him and let you know. How can I contact you?'

'You can send a message to me at the Hotel Continental.'

'What a fancy place!' He grinned. 'I'll send you a message as soon as I've spoken to Anton.'

Rosie jumped out of the wheelbarrow and joined Lottie, tail wagging.

'Thank you, Josef. I really appreciate it.'

## Chapter Twenty-Five

LOTTIE TOLD Mrs Moore about her conversation with Josef when she and Rosie returned to the hotel.

'Well done, you've already made some progress, Lottie! It doesn't look good for Prince Manfred, does it? I don't know how Boris can believe he's innocent if the button from his jacket was found at the crime scene.'

'There could be an innocent explanation for it.'

'I don't know what, though.'

'I'm looking forward to speaking to Anton, the waiter. He refused to serve Dr Fischer his food, then claimed to have heard a shout in the garden when he was walking there between half past nine and quarter to ten.'

'You think he could be the murderer?'

'He was in the grounds of the palace at the time of the doctor's death, so it's a possibility.'

'It is, isn't it? And that detective was fairly dismissive when you told him about the interaction between Anton and Dr Fischer. There could be something in it, however.'

'Hopefully I'll have a better idea once I've spoken to Anton.'

'In the meantime, I suppose we'd better speak to the other guests about the evening. I'm not sure it's worth our while, given the evidence against Prince Manfred, but we told Boris we'd look into it. We're probably wasting our time, aren't we?'

'We might not be. Who shall we speak to first?'

'I can't say I relish the idea of speaking to any of them. But let's try Countess von Friedensberg first. We can call on her after lunch.'

'That sounds like a good plan. Where's Barty?'

'He's gone to find a park to sit in where he can read his book of poetry.'

'I see.' It sounded like a respectable way to pass the time, but Lottie wasn't convinced it was true.

COUNTESS MARIE VON Friedensberg lived in a grand, five-storey townhouse on Vienna's picturesque ring road. The house was within walking distance of Lottie and Mrs Moore's hotel.

On arrival, they were shown into a perfumed grand salon cluttered with polished furniture, gilt-edged paintings, mirrors, vases, ornaments and trinkets. The red-haired countess was dressed in rose pink silk and reclined on a velvet chaise longue.

'How lovely of you to call on me, Mrs Moore, and what a delight it is to see your assistant and your jolly little dog, too. You've brightened my day.'

'I'm pleased to hear it, Countess.'

'Please be seated.' She gestured at a pair of easy chairs fringed with tassels. 'Would you like some grapes?'

'No, thank you.'

They watched as the countess pulled off a grape for herself and pushed it between her pink lips. 'I still can't comprehend what's happened,' she said once she'd consumed it. 'Prince

Manfred a murderer! I never would have thought he would do such a thing. He always seemed so pleasant, but perhaps we never truly know someone.'

'I agree,' said Mrs Moore. 'We think we know someone and then it transpires we don't know them at all.'

'Do you think the prince did it?' asked the countess.

'I think he must have done. A button from his jacket was found at the scene of the murder.'

'Was it? Then he must have done it. And he was conducting a love affair with Catherine Fischer! That came as a surprise.'

'It did indeed,' said Mrs Moore.

'I was a little upset when I found out about the affair because, between you and me, Prince Manfred and I held a lot of affection for each other.'

'Did you?' Lottie could hear the sharpness in Mrs Moore's tone.

'Yes. We met up in all sorts of exotic places and had great fun together.' Lottie felt sorry for Mrs Moore having to listen to such an admission. 'I did once fancy he might choose me as his wife,' continued the countess. 'I'm descended from European nobility and he's royalty, of course, so we're well matched. But it seems he preferred a common Englishwoman all along! What a mistake he made and look where it's got him! It wouldn't surprise me if Catherine took part in the crime, too. I think she and the prince wanted Dr Fischer out of the way. Some people are so selfish, aren't they? They will happily murder someone just so they can get what they want in life. Here, doggy, doggy!' She called over to Rosie, but the corgi remained sitting by Lottie's chair. 'Is she not friendly?' asked the countess.

'Sometimes,' replied Lottie, aware there were few people Rosie was reluctant to say hello to.

'How odd. Dogs usually adore me.' The countess helped

herself to another grape. 'Anyway, I shall have to use the murder plot in my next book.'

'But don't you write romance novels?' asked Mrs Moore.

'Yes, there will be romance. The story will be about a Bavarian prince and a psychoanalyst's wife who are so obsessively in love with each other that they conspire to murder the psychoanalyst so they can live happily ever after together. But then the prince is tried for murder and the psychoanalyst's wife dies of a broken heart when he is sent to the gallows.'

'Goodness, that's not a very cheery romance story.'

'It's not. It's a tragedy like Romeo and Juliet.'

'I can't imagine Prince Manfred and Mrs Fischer being happy about a story which is so obviously about them.'

'They should have thought about that before they began their affair. The story has a moral. Forbidden love always ends in heartache and death.'

'Does it?'

'Yes. Some of the time, anyway. In my story, the pair of them give into temptation and are therefore punished.'

'I suppose there's a possibility Prince Manfred didn't commit murder,' ventured Lottie. 'His interpreter and friend, Boris, is convinced he's innocent.'

The countess scowled. 'He's still loyal to the prince, then. None of us like to think a friend could be a murderer.'

'I'm wondering if there's a possibility someone else could have carried out the crime,' said Mrs Moore.

'Such as who?'

'I don't know. Mr Smallwood, for example.'

'Why would he do that?'

'Maybe there was a disagreement between Dr Fischer and Mr Smallwood which we don't know about.'

The countess narrowed her eyes. 'And what makes you say that?'

'It's just an idea.'

'I think it's wrong to have suspicions about people when you barely know them.'

'It's not very charitable, is it? But I'm just trying to establish whether someone else murdered Dr Fischer.'

The countess sighed. 'I wouldn't waste your time thinking about it, Mrs Moore. The detective knows what he's doing, and I think the evidence against the prince is obvious. I think Mrs Fischer should be arrested too, because she must have had something to do with it. How could her lover murder her husband without her knowing he was planning to do so? Perhaps I'm wrong, but I think she must have known something.'

'How well did you know Dr and Mrs Fischer?'

'Not very well.'

'Had you met them before the fateful evening?'

'No. I knew of them, though. Everyone in Vienna had heard of Dr Fischer.'

'Do you really think Mrs Fischer is capable of colluding with Prince Manfred to murder her husband?'

'No. But she must have done. She must have been obsessively in love with him and therefore did whatever he asked of her.'

'And you didn't see them in the garden when you went out for some air?'

'No.'

'You didn't hear anything?'

'No.'

'Apparently, a waiter at the palace heard the raised voice of a man between half past nine and quarter to ten.'

'Did he? Well, that sounds interesting. Come to think of it... yes, I think I might have heard a shout at around that time too.'

Lottie wondered if the countess had only just decided on this.

'Did you really?' asked Mrs Moore.

'Yes, I'm sure of it now.'

'What sort of shout was it?'

'Someone in pain. As if they'd just been hit over the head with a piece of rock.'

'Have you told the police about this?'

'Not yet, but thank you for the reminder, Mrs Moore. I shall inform Detective Inspector Berger.'

## Chapter Twenty-Six

'WHAT A DETESTABLE WOMAN,' said Mrs Moore after they left the countess's home. 'And to think she once entertained the idea of marrying Prince Manfred! I really am tired of hearing about the man. I'm quite tempted to tell Boris I have no interest in helping clear the prince's name. But...'

'What?'

'There's a possibility he's innocent, isn't there? A tiny possibility. And for as long as that fragment of doubt is there, then I suppose we should continue with our enquiries. For Boris's sake. Not Prince Manfred's.'

Lottie nodded in agreement.

'Who shall we speak to next?' asked her employer.

Lottie pulled Boris's map out of her bag. 'It looks like Catherine Fischer lives close by,' she said. 'But you don't have to speak to her, Mrs Moore. I can do it alone if you prefer.'

Mrs Moore sighed. 'No, it's fine. If she's innocent of her husband's murder, then I feel a little sorry for her. And as for Prince Manfred... she did me a favour by having an affair with him. She stopped my affection for him in its tracks. So I suppose I should thank her for that. I won't actually thank her, of course. But you know what I mean.'

'She probably regrets the affair.'

'I hope she does!'

CATHERINE FISCHER'S home was a short walk along the ring road. Although the house was a little smaller than the countess's, it was still a grand, wealthy home. Two cats sat on the steps as they approached the front door. Lottie put Rosie on her lead.

Inside, the house was dimly lit, and the curtains were drawn. The housekeeper led them to the library and Rosie tried to lunge at a cat they met on the way.

'It's very kind of you to visit me, Mrs Moore,' said Mrs Fischer weakly. She sat in a chair by the fireplace. She was dressed in black and her face was pale. She looked older than Lottie remembered, and not quite as pretty. Her husband's death had clearly taken its toll. 'No one else wants to visit me at the moment,' she continued. 'They think I'm treacherous.'

'Oh,' responded Mrs Moore, clearly uncertain how to reply. They sat in two chairs opposite Mrs Fischer and Rosie tugged on the lead, keen to visit a cat which sat on a writing table.

Countless books lined the shelves on the walls. Lottie could make out the titles on some of them and deduced they were serious academic texts about the brain and the mind.

'So I appreciate you visiting me,' said Mrs Fischer. 'I've had so little company since Felix died. It really has been miserable. And I realise I've made a lot of mistakes, but this situation I find myself in now is purgatory. My husband is dead and a man whom I care deeply about is locked in a prison cell!' She emitted a sob.

'There, there,' said Mrs Moore. 'You won't always feel this terrible.'

'I hope not.'

'One day, things will seem brighter again. We received a visit from Boris yesterday who's quite convinced his master is not a murderer. He's asked us to look into things.'

'Why?'

'My clever companion, Lottie, has a talent for detective work.'

'Really?' Lottie couldn't decide if Mrs Fischer was pleased or wary about this information.

'Yes. So we're going to do what Boris asked and see where it gets us.'

'Very well.'

'Do you think Prince Manfred is the murderer?' asked Mrs Moore.

'No! He wouldn't hurt a fly!'

'Which is something Boris alluded to. Apparently, he once spent a day trying to fix a fly's broken wing.'

'That's exactly the sort of man he is! It's all so terribly unfair!'

'I suppose matters haven't been helped by the discovery of the button from his jacket at the crime scene.'

'No, that was very unfortunate.'

'Do you know how it got there?'

'I have no idea! I think someone must have put it there!'

'How?'

'I think they must have cut the button off his jacket when he wasn't looking.'

'But how would they even have managed that?'

'I don't know! But that button must have been planted there to make it look like he murdered my husband!'

Mrs Moore gave Lottie a glance which suggested she

didn't believe this story. 'So, who do you think murdered your husband, Mrs Fischer?'

'Call me Catherine, please. I think a madman broke into the gardens.'

'So you don't think it could have been any of the other guests?'

'No. I don't see why Mr Smallwood would have harmed him and the countess adored him.'

'Did she?'

'Yes! She was one of his favourite patients.'

'She was one of your husband's patients?'

'Yes. I'm not supposed to know that. It was all meant to be confidential, you see. But Felix couldn't help telling me who'd been in to visit him. I swore not to tell anyone else, and I never did. Not even Manfred. But now my husband is dead, I don't see that it's a problem to share some of the things he told me.'

'So what did he say about the countess?'

'He didn't tell me what they discussed, but he did say she visited him each week and that he enjoyed helping her.'

Lottie wondered why the countess had decided not to tell them this information.

'I'm surprised she hasn't visited me yet, because she and I were good friends,' continued Catherine.

'You were?'

'Yes. She didn't mention she was visiting my husband. She kept her secrets, and I kept mine. However, we used to enjoy afternoon tea together and discuss current affairs. But now I feel as though I've lost a friend. As well as a husband. That's why I'm so grateful you've visited me today. So thoughtful and kind of you.'

'Why do you think a madman would murder your husband?'

'I don't know. I've no idea how the mind of a madman works. My husband would have been able to tell you, but he's no longer here. The trouble with a madman is that he behaves irrationally, so no one can know why he did it or, in fact, what he's planning next. Isn't it scary to think he's roaming around the streets of Vienna and instead the police have arrested the innocent prince?'

'If a murdering madman is roaming the streets, then it's scary indeed.'

'Mr Smallwood did such a beautiful performance. I feel so pleased that my husband could enjoy something so wonderful on his very last evening.'

'Although not beautiful enough for him to stay and enjoy the entire performance,' commented Mrs Moore.

'No. Although I must add that Felix and I had enjoyed a performance by Percy before.'

'Is that so?'

'Yes, he visited our home last year to perform for our guests.'

'Did your husband know Percy well?'

'Not very well. Just well enough to invite him here one evening. I have to say that I thought Percy would be a little friendlier, given that we had met him before.'

'Did you not find him friendly the other evening?'

'No, I found him rather sullen. He rebuffed my attempts to make conversation with him. I don't know why. Perhaps I did something to offend him?'

'Was he the same with your husband?'

'Yes, in fact, Felix remarked on it. I put it down to Percy being a musician. Creative people can be very temperamental, so I chose not to worry about it.'

'At dinner there was a waiter called Anton who refused to serve your husband,' said Lottie. 'Do you know why?'

'Refused to serve him? How rude. I hope the prince has fired him!'

'You don't know anything about the waiter?'

'No. Felix didn't mention him.'

'I hope you don't mind me asking this,' said Lottie. 'But did your husband discover the affair between you and Prince Manfred?'

Catherine pursed her lips. 'That's quite an impertinent question,' she said. Then she turned to Mrs Moore. 'You should ask your assistant to remember her manners.'

'Lottie didn't mean to be rude,' said Mrs Moore. 'And I'm afraid it's something which everyone is wondering. I know the question makes you uncomfortable, but the tragic murder of your husband has made things which were once private, not so private.'

Catherine gave a sigh. 'I don't see why I should have to answer such questions, but if I try to avoid them, then people will assume I'm trying to hide something. So in answer to your question... yes, he did find out. And as for the button... I do know how it got there. I told you a fib.'

'Why?'

'Oh, because everything is such a mess! I don't know what to say.'

'The truth?'

'Alright then. Felix did find out about the affair that evening but it was something he'd suspected for a while. He discovered a love letter which the prince sent me from Cairo and he got angry about it. I explained it was a friendly letter and nothing more. I think my words calmed him a little. And then, at the palace, well, the prince and I hadn't seen each other for a few months and we were desperate to find some time together. The prince decided on a plan to sneak out of the music recital. He hoped everyone would be too engrossed in the performance to notice. I had some reservations about the plan, but I was so keen to spend some time with him I went along with it.'

Lottie noticed Mrs Moore's expression was stony.

'I found the prince in the garden, and we enjoyed a stroll together,' said Catherine. 'There was no one else about and we had the most wonderful time catching up on each other's news. The prince wanted to play a game of hide and seek in the maze. He can be so playful sometimes! So that's what we did. He was the hider, and I was the seeker. He was very good at hiding and I crept about the place, quite desperate to catch him out. Eventually, I saw some movement in a corner and prepared myself for the ambush. I pounced on him immediately and realised too late that it was my husband! I couldn't hide my surprise, and that's what gave me away. I tried ever so hard to convince Felix he was the person I had intended to pounce on and I think he almost believed me. But then Manfred, the silly fool, appeared from around the corner and my husband realised what the game was. He chased after the prince.'

'He *chased* him?'

'Yes. Manfred took off and Felix ran after him. I called out for them both to stop, but they ignored me. I managed to leave the maze in the end, and I found them outside it, both arguing. Felix looked so desperately hurt. After shouting at Manfred, he then marched off. I wanted to leave him, but Manfred insisted on following him. He told me he was desperate to make amends with his friend. I couldn't see how he'd be able to do it because I could see how hurt my husband was. I told Manfred that Felix would need to calm down before anyone spoke to him. But Manfred wouldn't listen, and off he went and followed him.

'I sat on a bench and wept. What else could I do? I realised how foolish I'd been. A short while later, Manfred returned. He told me he'd spoken to Felix, but my husband had been too upset to listen. Apparently, he had called Manfred every name under the sun.'

'I'm not surprised.'

'And so Manfred told me he had to walk away and leave him.'

'Alive?'

'Of course! You can't possibly think that Manfred would murder his friend. In fact, I could have imagined my husband murdering Manfred! He was so angry and upset. Manfred was very upset, too. We all were. We decided to leave Felix for a bit, and I resolved to find him later. I decided I'd wait until he was calmer and talk to him then. But sadly, that moment never came! A short while later, I heard his body had been found, and I was distraught! I blame myself.'

'Why?'

'Because if I hadn't agreed to sneak out of the performance with Manfred, then my husband wouldn't have followed us, and he wouldn't have met his death! I can only imagine he was wandering around the Roman ruin feeling sorry for himself, and that's when the madman struck. Oh, it's so desperately sad!'

'Yes it is,' said Mrs Moore.

Although there was little doubt Catherine Fischer was upset, Lottie wondered if her story could be believed. 'When you sat on the bench and wept,' she asked, 'could you still see your husband and Prince Manfred?'

'No, they were out of sight. That's when they must have been at the Roman ruin. And that's when the button would have fallen off Manfred's jacket.'

'How long were they out of your sight for?'

'I really don't know! When you're upset like that, time loses all significance. It could have been two minutes or it could have been ten minutes. I really couldn't tell you.'

'Did you notice the missing button on Prince Manfred's jacket when he returned?'

'No. I didn't look at his buttons. My eyes were swimming with tears!'

# Chapter Twenty-Seven

'So what do you think, Lottie?' asked Mrs Moore once they'd left Mrs Fischer's dingy home. 'Could Catherine Fischer be a murderess?'

'She could be,' said Lottie. 'Or she may not be. I'm struggling to decide.'

'It's odd that the only explanation she can give is a madman,' said Mrs Moore. 'You'd think she'd have some thoughts about who murdered her husband. Unless she did it herself. And what did Countess von Friedensberg say about the Fischers? She'd heard of them but had never met them before the fateful evening. She lied to us.'

'Presumably because she didn't want to admit she was a patient of Dr Fischer's. But she could have bent the truth a little bit, rather than flatly denying she'd ever met them. And Catherine Fischer claimed they were friends! I don't know why she denied that.'

'She's clearly decided to distance herself from the pair. And she was quite unflattering about Catherine, even though they'd supposedly once been friends. Perhaps she felt betrayed by her because of the affair with Prince Manfred. I don't like being lied to. The countess must think we're stupid!'

'She's lying because she's trying to protect herself,' said Lottie. 'And somehow we need to find out why.'

AFTER A STOP for coffee at the Mozart Café, Lottie, Mrs Moore and Rosie arrived at the Imperial Academy of Music and the Performing Arts.

'This is where Percival Smallwood told us he practices,' said Mrs Moore, surveying the smart facade with countless arched windows.

Inside, Mrs Moore mentioned the composer's name to a man behind the desk, and he led them down a wooden staircase to a basement corridor. The air was warm and musty and the lighting weak. Eventually they reached a door and beyond it came the sound of a piano. The receptionist nodded and went on his way. Lottie and Mrs Moore remained at the door, wary of interrupting the composer. The same phrase was being played over and over on the piano, as if Percy were trying to perfect it.

'We'll have to go in,' whispered Mrs Moore. 'But I can't imagine him being happy about it.'

She knocked, but no answer came. Clearly the composer was too focused on his work to hear.

'Here goes...' said Mrs Moore, turning the door handle. It swung open to reveal a windowless, wood-panelled room. A single lightbulb hanging from the ceiling provided light.

The music abruptly stopped.

'What is it?' Percy sat at the piano in the centre of the room. 'You know you're not supposed to disturb me!'

'It's Mrs Moore, Miss Sprigg and Rosie,' said Mrs Moore.

'What?' Percy pulled his spectacles from his jacket and put them on. 'Oh hello. What a surprise to see you here. This isn't a good time, I'm afraid. I'm in the middle of a difficult passage.'

'We're sorry to disturb you, Percy. But this will only take five minutes.'

'Will it?' He got up from the piano stool and began pacing the floor. 'Perhaps some inspiration will strike me if I take a break. It is possible to sweat over something so much that nothing more comes out. A bit like squeezing a rag which is bone dry.' He stopped and faced them, his hands on his hips. 'What do you wish to discuss, Mrs Moore?'

'We had a chat with Mrs Fischer.'

'Did you? How is she?'

'She's very upset and wracked with guilt.'

'I'm not surprised. Do you think she murdered her husband?'

'What a question! I don't know, I...'

'I think she could have done. It was probably a plan between her and the Bavarian prince. He's clearly guilty and I imagine she helped him.'

'The prince's lifelong friend, Boris, insists he's innocent.'

'That's no great surprise. He needs to realise what sort of man he's working for. The prince hasn't even paid me for my performance the other evening!'

'No, really?'

'Apparently he was too grief-stricken to cough up at the time. Boris told me I'd be paid the following day but then the prince got arrested and I don't know when I'll see my money.'

'Oh dear. Is it causing a problem for you?' asked Mrs Moore.

'No, no. I'm fine. But it's the principle.'

'It certainly is.'

'If there's one thing I absolutely *hate*, it's people who think they can get away without paying me.'

'It's rather rude of them.'

'It's more than rude! It's offensive!'

'Absolutely.'

'And it's arrogant. They seem to think that the honour of playing for them is enough! And there is no honour in it, I'm afraid. And even if there was, it doesn't pay the bills.'

'No.'

'So I have little sympathy for Prince Manfred.'

'I can imagine. There's something I'd like to clear up, if you don't mind.'

'Go on. Is it quick?'

'Yes. Mrs Fischer mentioned she didn't find you particularly friendly the other evening.'

'Did she? What a strange thing to say.'

'I wondered if there had been a disagreement between you and the Fischers.'

'No. Why would there be? I'd never met them before.'

'That's not what Mrs Fischer told us.'

'Oh?' He pulled a baffled expression.

'She said you performed for them at their home last year.'

'That's right, I did.'

'But you said you'd never met them before.'

He gave an uneasy smile. 'I think we attribute slightly different meanings to our words, Mrs Moore. When I say *met*, I mean meeting someone properly and having a proper conversation with them. Much as we are now. When I performed for them last year, only a few words were exchanged. So I didn't know them at all.'

'I see. For a moment, I wondered if you were denying knowing them.'

'I didn't know them. Perhaps that's why Mrs Fischer interpreted my behaviour as rude the other evening. Not half as rude as walking out in the middle of a recital, but we all have different standards, I suppose. So for Mrs Fischer to describe me as unfriendly, well I call that a complete nonsense! Perhaps it's unfair of me to say that about a grieving widow. But if she's a scheming murderess, then I have no regrets about saying it at all! Is there anything else?'

'I was wondering if Dr Fischer and Mrs Fischer had done anything to upset you.'

'Walking out of my performance.'

'Before then. Perhaps when you performed for them last year?'

'No. Apart from the small matter of Dr Fischer not paying me for my performance.'

'Another one who didn't cough up?'

'Exactly. Scandalous, isn't it? Anyway, I'm not sure why you're asking me these questions, Mrs Moore.'

'I'm just interested and trying to make sense of what happened the other evening.'

'Aren't we all? But it sounds like the police have got the right idea. The detective has arrested the prince and hopefully soon he'll arrest Mrs Fischer, too. Then we can all sleep safely in our beds. Now you must excuse me, I need to get back to my work.'

MOMENTS after they left the room, they heard the piano again. Percy was back at work, playing the same sequence over and over.

'He's an odd man, isn't he, Lottie?' said Mrs Moore as they walked away.

'He certainly is. He claimed he'd never met the Fischers before, then came up with a strange definition of the word. I don't think he would've admitted to us he'd performed for them before if we hadn't already found it out from Catherine Fischer. What's he hiding?'

'If only we knew.'

## Chapter Twenty-Eight

MRS MOORE WAS tired by the time they returned to the hotel late in the afternoon. 'I need a lie down, Lottie. Speaking to unpleasant people is quite exhausting, isn't it? I'll see you for dinner in an hour.'

Lottie felt the need for some quiet time, too. She went to her room with Rosie and made herself comfortable in the chair by the window with her book of detective stories. She read one page before there was a knock at the door.

She opened it. 'Barty?'

'Hello Lottie, Auntie's not in there with you, is she?'

'No. Why are you whispering?'

'In case Auntie's in there.'

'She's not.'

'Good.'

'You'd better come in then.'

Barty stepped in and perched on the bed next to Rosie. 'You're jolly good at keeping everything nice and tidy in here, aren't you, Lottie? I've managed to make a complete mess of my room already. Tidiness doesn't come naturally to me.'

'It doesn't come naturally to many people,' said Lottie,

returning to her chair by the window. 'Sometimes you just need to make an effort.'

Barty laughed and slapped his knee. 'You don't mince your words, do you? You're right. I should put in some effort. It's such hard work, though. Anyway, I didn't call on you to discuss my untidy habits. I need to have a word with you out of the earshot of dear old Auntie.'

Lottie's heart sank. 'What have you done?'

'Nothing at all. I've not done anything. I just appear to have found myself in a little scrape.'

'And you want me to help you?'

'Now, let's not jump the gun. I need to explain a few things first.'

Lottie groaned. 'You told Mrs Moore you'd turned over a new leaf.'

'I have! This latest episode is really just a most unfortunate turn of events.'

'Perhaps you'd better explain it to me then. I can't promise to help, though.'

'We'll get to that bit later. I was terribly bored when you and Auntie Roberta went to the palace the other evening and I asked the barman here at the hotel about the best places to enjoy an evening drink. He recommended a nice little place called the Mozart Bar, and that's where I settled myself for a quiet evening, enjoying the ambience of Vienna as one does.'

'I think I've seen that place. Is it next to the Mozart Cafe?'

'I believe it is. They like Mozart here, don't they? Anyway, there I was minding my own business when an attractive young lady struck up a conversation with me. She's a delightful Austrian girl called Anna and, as luck would have it, she speaks perfect English. Which just as well because my knowledge of German is scant, to say the least. Latin, Greek and French are no problem for me, but German sounds like a completely foreign language. Which I suppose it is! Anyway, we got along famously and I happened to bump into her again yesterday and today. Obviously, it's been very helpful to make a friend in this large city where I don't know a soul apart from you and Auntie. And so, naturally, I've been rather enthusiastic about the friendship.'

'And?'

'Well... It appears that Anna has fallen hopelessly in love with me.'

'Oh.'

'So much so that she's considering calling off her wedding to the son of a well-known Viennese financier.'

'She's engaged to be *married*?'

'Yes, but it's important for you to know I didn't realise this when we struck up our first conversation. And besides, I was merely being friendly. I'm on my own here in Vienna and I was keen to make new chums. Now, quite clearly, matters have got out of hand. She was all set to announce to her father this evening that she plans to elope with me to England.'

'*What*?'

'I know. It's a little excessive, isn't it? She's clearly fallen head over heels for me. I managed to persuade her to hold off from speaking to her father for a day or two. But I haven't got long.'

'To do what?'

'To make her fall *out* of love with me! Things have got a little out of control. All I did was make a small snowball and now it's rolling down a hill, getting rapidly larger and faster as we speak!'

'Are you asking me to stop the snowball?'

Barty pulled an endearing face which presumably worked on some ladies. But Lottie had known him since he was fifteen, and it wasn't an expression which worked on her.

'I can't promise to help you with anything,' she said, suspecting Barty had done his best to charm Anna before discovering she was engaged. 'But what crackpot idea do you have in mind?'

'Crackpot? It's a sensible idea! And I think it would be quite easy.'

'Are you sure?'

'Oh yes. All I need you to do is pretend you're my sister.'

'Oh no! And do what?'

'And then meet with Anna and tell her what a rotten scoundrel I am. Tell her she'll only end up broken-hearted and that she should stick to her plan of marrying... whoever that chap is she's supposed to be marrying. I can't remember his name. That wouldn't be too difficult to do, would it?'

'So you want me to get you out of this mess?'

'I wouldn't quite call it that. But yes.'

Lottie felt sorry for Anna. She'd fallen for Barty, but the feeling wasn't reciprocated. 'If I agree to do this,' she said. 'Where would I meet her?'

'In the Mozart Bar at nine o'clock tomorrow evening.'

'You've already arranged for me to meet her?'

'No. That's the time I've arranged to meet her and you just need to turn up in my place.'

Lottie laughed. 'I can't imagine she'll be very happy about that!'

'No, she won't be. But that's because I'm a scoundrel. That's what she needs to think, anyway. I'm not actually a scoundrel. It's all been a terrible misunderstanding.'

'You seem to find yourself in a lot of misunderstandings, Barty.'

'I do! It's most unfair. So will you do it?'

'Meet Anna and tell her you're a scoundrel?'

'Yes. Tell her I'm a good-for-nothing rapscallion. A cad and a bounder. Tell her she should have nothing more to do with me.'

'Do you think she'll listen?'

'Yes. Because you're my sister. For the purposes of this exercise. Oh, and you'll have to use another name for yourself. Charity Farquhar.'

'*What?*'

'Teddy Farquhar's sister.'

'Who's Teddy?'

'Me! There was no way I was going to tell Anna my real name. She'd soon learn that Bartholomew Buckley-Phipps had been sent to Vienna in disgrace.'

'Would she?'

'Yes. Word spreads quickly when you're the son of a lord, I've learnt that the hard way. Teddy's the name I've used lots of times before.'

'Under what circumstances?'

'Circumstances when I've had to lie about who I am. Now, Anna knows I'm in Vienna with my sister, Charity, so she pretty much already knows you.'

Lottie shook her head. 'No, I don't think I can go through with this, Barty.'

'But you must! Otherwise, the poor girl will ruin her future!'

'But you're asking me to tell her lies about who you are. And who I am too! I'm hopeless at telling lies and I don't enjoy doing it.'

'It's just a little white lie, Lottie. Anna will be none the wiser! She'll be upset, of course, but that's necessary if she's to be saved. Think of yourself as saving her, Lottie.'

'From your lies and manipulation?'

He recoiled. 'Ouch, that's hurtful.'

'I don't understand why you felt the need to make friends with Anna. You could have just kept to yourself when you visited that bar.'

'Honestly, I tried! Perhaps I have a weakness for a pretty

face, but I did my best. How did I know she would then wish to call off her wedding and elope with me?'

Lottie sighed. It was a tricky predicament. 'Why don't you tell Anna yourself?'

'She wouldn't listen to me! At just one sight of me, she falls into a swoon all over again and doesn't heed a word I say.'

'Really?'

'I swear it!' Lottie suspected the real reason he didn't want to speak to Anna himself was because he was too scared to do it.

She felt another pang of sympathy for poor Anna who seemed to have difficulty choosing a suitable man for herself. She couldn't be particularly happy about her choice of future husband if she'd fallen so quickly for Barty. Perhaps it wasn't a good idea for her to marry the Viennese financier's son, but pinning her hopes on Barty would be a mistake.

'I'll think about it.'

'Only think about it?'

'I have to think about whether to meet Anna or not. I don't like the thought of making up stories.'

'I don't mind you saying bad things about me, Lottie. The badder the better. I need her to fall out of love with me!'

'I'll find that bit quite easy.'

'Oh.'

'What I don't want to do is tell her my name is Charity Farquhar.'

'It's not a bad name.'

'It's not my name. I like to be honest with people.'

Barty gave a sigh. 'Well, I can only hope you'll agree to it, Lottie. Otherwise, it's going to end up in a dreadful mess if she tells her father. Honesty isn't always the best policy, you know.'

'You could help yourself by being honest now and again,

Barty. I'm sure you'd find yourself caught up in fewer misunderstandings.'

'Perhaps.' He sighed. 'Well, whatever you decide to do, please don't mention this to Auntie Roberta, will you? She'll be so disappointed in me.'

'You're right. She will be. I thought you'd been busy reading your book of poetry for the past few days.'

'Yes, that's what I've told people just to keep them happy. I'm trying my hardest to turn over a new leaf, Lottie, but I don't seem able to manage it.'

## Chapter Twenty-Nine

LOTTIE RECEIVED A MESSAGE FROM JOSEF, the gardener, at breakfast the following morning.

'He says Anton, the waiter, is happy to speak to me today at eleven o'clock,' she told Mrs Moore.

'Excellent! It will be interesting to hear what he has to say.' She took a sip of tea. 'On reflection, I enjoyed our little bit of detective work yesterday afternoon. We discovered Countess von Friedensberg lied about knowing Dr Fischer and Percival Smallwood tried to claim he hadn't met him when he had.'

'They both denied knowing him before the gathering at the palace. I wonder why?'

'I hope we can find out. Very mysterious isn't it? Talking of mysteries, where's Barty this morning?' Mrs Moore glanced around the restaurant through her lorgnette. 'If he doesn't hurry along, he's going to miss breakfast. I hope he isn't just lying about in bed. He's done so well over the past few days, hasn't he?' Lottie gave an unconvincing nod. 'It would be a shame if he lapsed into his old layabout ways.'

Lottie wanted to tell Mrs Moore about Barty's apparent misunderstanding with the young Austrian woman, but she knew her employer would be bitterly disappointed to hear it. And Barty had sworn her to secrecy, too. She had to make her mind up whether to help him or not.

LATER THAT MORNING, Lottie arrived with Rosie at Schönbrunn Palace. She didn't have to worry about a protracted conversation with the guards because Josef was waiting at the gate for her.

'Thank you for speaking to Anton,' she said to him as they walked across the quadrangle towards the palace. 'Hopefully, he'll be able to explain to me why he didn't want to serve Dr Fischer.'

'He's explained it to me,' said Josef.

'Really? What did he say?'

'I'll let him tell you himself. Although I'll have to translate. He doesn't speak much English.'

They walked through the colonnade and turned left. Josef led her to the far end of the palace building where a walled area had been built around a tradesman's entrance. Josef disappeared through the door and returned a short while later with the brown-haired and freckled waiter Lottie recognised from the dinner.

He smiled at her and said something to Josef.

'Anton remembers you,' said Josef.

'Good. I remember him too.'

Rosie sniffed the waiter and received a pat on the head. Then Anton lit a thin cigarette and began talking.

'He says he used to work for Dr Fischer and his wife at their home on Schubertring,' said Josef.

'Where's that?'

'It's part of the ring road which is named after the composer Schubert.'

'Another composer? It seems quite a few of them have

lived in Vienna.'

'Yes, they have. Schubert is particularly special because he was born here. So was the elder Strauss. But they all lived here, Mozart, Beethoven, Haydn, Mahler... there's a long list. It is why Vienna is the city of music. And we've gone completely off the topic now.' He grinned.

'So we have, sorry about that. Please can you ask Anton how long ago he worked for the Fischers?'

Josef asked Anton, then translated again. 'Three years ago. He was taken on as a junior servant and he had ambitions to be a butler. But after a while, Dr Fischer falsely accused him of stealing silver. Apparently, it was one of the maids who did it, but because she was a favourite of Dr Fischer's, he refused to believe she would do such a thing. So instead, he made Anton take the blame and dismissed him.'

'Oh no, that's awful.'

'And Dr Fischer told him he would ensure that he would never work anywhere in Vienna again. So he told all his friends not to employ him and all his patients too.'

'How spiteful!'

'Anton struggled to find work for a long time, but last year he was taken on as a waiter at a restaurant. Luckily, the manager didn't listen to Dr Fischer's lies and gave Anton a chance. He got the job here for this week because the restaurant manager knows Prince Manfred.'

'I see. I understand now why Anton was so upset about having to wait on Dr Fischer the other evening.'

'Apparently, he didn't know Dr Fischer was a guest at Prince Manfred's dinner until he entered the room with the soup. He wanted to leave immediately but realised it would create too much of a fuss. So instead he asked his colleague to wait on the doctor instead.'

'Did Dr Fischer recognise him?'

Josef asked Anton this before replying, 'Yes. He noticed

him and kept staring at him in a confrontational manner.'

Lottie nodded. 'I noticed that. Did he speak to Dr Fischer at all?'

Josef asked Anton, and the waiter responded with a shake of his head. 'Nein.'

'I noticed Anton and his colleague were laughing together after Percival Smallwood's performance finished,' said Lottie. 'Can you ask him if he remembers what made him laugh?'

'He says it was a joke between them,' said Josef after putting the question to Anton. 'They thought the composer had funny mannerisms and were amused by people leaving and falling asleep.'

'That was quite funny.' Lottie nodded in agreement. 'And when Anton finished work for the evening, he walked through the palace grounds?'

'Yes, on his way home.'

'And what time was that?'

'He left after the music recital.'

'About half past nine, then. Can you ask Anton if he saw Dr Fischer in the palace grounds before his death that evening?'

'He didn't see him.'

'Did he see anyone else?'

'No one else.'

'But he heard a shout?'

'Yes, between half past nine and a quarter to ten.'

'Does he think the shout could have come from the attack on Dr Fischer?'

'He doesn't know.'

'But it must have done, mustn't it? Who else could have made that noise?'

Josef discussed this with Anton and then said, 'He agrees it was probably Dr Fischer, but he doesn't want to say for certain because there's no evidence.'

'That sounds sensible.'

'And he has told the police all about it too.'

'Another sensible thing to do.' Lottie turned to Anton. 'Thank you for talking to me.'

JOSEF ESCORTED Lottie and Rosie back to the gate.

'Do you think Anton could have harmed Dr Fischer?' Lottie asked.

'No. Never!'

'But he was out of work for a long time because of him.'

'Yes, he was, and he had every right to be angry with him. But I don't believe he would do something like that. And he's found work now, so it's all forgotten about.'

'But perhaps he came across him in the gardens and confronted him? Perhaps the two argued, and he lost his temper?'

'I can't imagine it.'

'How well do you know Anton?'

'Not very well.'

'So perhaps he is capable of such a thing?'

'I can't imagine it. But as you say, I don't know him very well. And besides, Prince Manfred has been arrested, hasn't he? Surely it must be him?'

'That's what everyone seems to think. Apart from Mrs Fischer. She thinks a madman did it.'

Josef laughed. 'A madman?'

'Have you seen a madman wandering around the palace gardens?'

'I haven't. Do you think Mrs Fischer has come up with that story because she's responsible?'

'It's possible.' Lottie sighed. 'At the moment, anything seems possible.'

LOTTIE RETURNED to the hotel and found Mrs Moore sitting with Boris in the lounge. Rosie ran up to greet them.

'Lottie! Do come and join us,' said Mrs Moore. 'Boris was just updating me on the latest developments.'

The interpreter got to his feet and gave Lottie a little bow.

'So what's happened?' asked Lottie, settling into an easy chair.

'Prince Manfred has been released from police custody,' said Boris. 'He's explained everything to Detective Inspector Berger and finally he believes him.'

'What's his explanation for his jacket button being found at the murder scene?' asked Lottie.

'He says Dr Fischer attacked him.'

Mrs Moore tutted. 'He's always blameless, isn't he?'

'Prince Manfred says he had to defend himself,' continued Boris. 'And it's quite believable that Dr Fischer attacked him because he'd just discovered that the prince was having an affair with his wife. It's a natural reaction from some people when they hear such news. Out of character, perhaps, but an understandable response. It's also understandable that the prince defended himself. He's not a violent man. Having known him since he was a boy, I can assure you of that.'

'So Prince Manfred maintains he had a scuffle with Dr Fischer at the Roman ruin and that's how the button came off his jacket,' said Mrs Moore.

'Yes. The prince tells me he noticed it was coming loose earlier in the day and he decided he would tell his valet about it.'

'Did he mention it to his valet?'

'Apparently not, he didn't have time. It was a busy day for him, which you know yourself, Mrs Moore. We did a tour of the gardens and then the prince was busy entertaining his guests.'

'I didn't notice any of his buttons coming loose.'

'Did you examine them closely?'

'Not very closely, no.'

'The important thing to remember is that Prince Manfred is admitting to a scuffle with Dr Fischer,' said Boris. 'If he had actually murdered him, then I don't believe he would admit to the scuffle.'

'But perhaps he's hoping that if he admits to the minor offence, he will then be presumed innocent of the serious one?' said Lottie.

'I don't think the prince's mind works like that. I think he was reluctant to admit to the scuffle because he worried everyone would assume he was a murderer.'

'I suppose Prince Manfred's explanation ties in with Mrs Fischer's story,' said Lottie.

'What did Mrs Fischer say?' asked Boris.

'She said she was playing hide and seek in the maze with Prince Manfred when her husband found them,' said Mrs Moore. 'He was understandably upset and chased after the prince, who ran off. When she found them, they were arguing, then Dr Fischer marched off. Apparently, Prince Manfred then followed him, and I imagine that's when they ended up at the Roman ruin. Mrs Fischer waited on a bench until the prince returned and told her he'd spoken to her husband but he'd been too upset to listen.'

'Did she mention a scuffle?'

'No. She doesn't appear to have witnessed one, and neither did Prince Manfred admit to one at the time. Clearly, the discovery of the button has forced him to admit their alter-cation became physical.'

Boris wiped his brow. 'So he could have murdered Dr Fischer? Perhaps not intentionally, but by mistake... No! I refuse to believe it. There may have been a scuffle, but I feel sure Manfred would have run away if there had been any hint of it becoming too serious.'

Mrs Moore sighed. 'We only have Prince Manfred's word for it. But it seems Detective Inspector Berger believes him because he's released him from custody now. So, if Prince Manfred is not the murderer, the question remains. Who did it?'

## Chapter Thirty-One

'I DON'T KNOW what to think now,' said Mrs Moore after Boris had left. 'It's all rather confusing. How did you get on with your gardener friend and the waiter, Lottie?'

Lottie told her about the conversation with Josef and Anton.

'Goodness, it sounds like Anton was treated poorly by Dr Fischer. And his story explains his refusal to serve the psycho-analyst at dinner. Well done, Lottie, you were extremely obser-vant to spot that.'

'It makes me wonder if Anton could be the murderer. Josef doesn't agree with me, but Anton has already admitted he heard shouts in the garden at around the time of Dr Fisch-er's murder. Perhaps Anton was actually at the scene of the shouting?'

'It's a thought, isn't it? It's rather risky for a young waiter to suddenly decide to murder a famous psychoanalyst, though.'

'But the more I think about it, the more convinced I am that it could be him,' said Lottie. 'He hadn't seen Dr Fischer for a long time and he hadn't been expecting to see him at the

151

dinner. He was clearly so angry when he saw him that he refused to serve him. Perhaps he left for home that evening still feeling angry and then he bumped into the doctor on the way? Perhaps Dr Fischer said something to him which angered him further and the provocation was too much to resist?'

'I agree with you. Lottie, there could be something in it. The young man has a motive, there's no doubt about it. So what do we do next? Should we mention it to Detective Inspector Berger?'

'I feel wary about doing that after I was threatened in Paris. And besides, Anton might be completely innocent.'

'It's a dilemma, isn't it? This sort of thing can be a dangerous business. You're dealing with someone who's prepared to murder another person. If they hear you've been talking to the police about them, then it could provoke a strong reaction. In an ideal world, Detective Inspector Berger will have interviewed all the staff and established that one of them is an angry former employee of Dr Fischer. In fact, he may have done that and may already be interested in Anton.'

'Hello!' They were interrupted by Barty bouncing towards them. 'I do believe it's lunchtime,' he said, rubbing his stomach. 'Are we having lunch?'

'Good idea, Barty,' said Mrs Moore. 'You missed breakfast, didn't you?'

'I did! I was too engrossed in my poetry book to notice the time.' He turned to Lottie. 'Have you decided whether you'd like to accompany me to the Mozart Bar this evening?'

Lottie opened, then closed her mouth, unsure how to respond.

'You're taking Lottie to the Mozart Bar?' asked Mrs Moore.

'Yes! We've been getting on like a house on fire, so I thought it would be fun. Lottie's like the long-lost sister I never had!'

'You have six sisters, Barty.'

'I mean a sister I actually like. So what do you say, Lottie? You don't have to, of course, if you don't want to. Don't feel I'm putting any pressure on you to say yes. The decision is entirely yours. I would just like to know if you think it's a good idea?' He held himself in a posture of anticipation, as if he couldn't move until she finally answered.

Lottie thought of the Austrian girl, Anna, and how she was on the verge of cancelling her wedding for Barty. Anna deserved to know the truth. 'Alright then.'

'Yippee!' Barty clapped his hands with glee.

'Do I get an invitation?' asked Mrs Moore.

'To the Mozart Bar? No, you're too aged for that sort of thing, Auntie.' He held out a hand to help her out of her chair.

'How rude, Barty!' She took his hand and stood up. 'I've a good mind to box your ears!'

Chapter Thirty-Two

At nine o'clock that evening, Lottie, Rosie and Barty stood on a street corner about fifty yards from the Mozart Bar. The sun had set behind Vienna's skyline, leaving the sky a fiery orange. The evening air was warm and the sound of music and laughter drifted from the cafes and bars around them.

'There it is, Lottie, see it?' Barty pointed down the street. 'It says *Mozart Bar* on the outside.'

'Yes, I see it. Thank you, Barty.'

'Now you can't miss Anna. She's a pretty little thing. Blonde bobbed hair, blue eyes. She'll be sitting at the table by the staircase. It's our table. Well, it *was* our table. Oh dear, poor Anna. I'm worried she's going to be dreadfully upset.'

'I'm worried about that too.'

'But she has to fall out of love with me, the situation can't continue. If she gets angry with you, just blame everything on me.'

'Oh, I intend to.'

'Alright then. I'll be pacing around that park across the

road. Come and find me there afterwards. Would you like me to mind Rosie?'

'Thank you, that would be helpful.' She handed him Rosie's lead, and he patted the corgi on the head.

'And when this is done, I'll arrange a treat as a thank you. How about a carriage ride around Vienna? I've seen the horses trotting around with those fine carriages behind them and I think it looks a lot of fun.'

'I like the sound of that.'

'Good. Alright then.' He took in a breath. 'I feel so terribly nervous for you, Lottie. Good luck!'

Lottie said goodbye to Rosie, then walked up to the Mozart Bar. Was she foolish for agreeing to do this for Barty? She probably was. But she also felt sorry for the girl he'd been leading on. She was owed an explanation.

She took a breath before stepping inside. The bar was hot and busy with young people in colourful dresses and smart suits. Lively chatter mingled with the music from a jazz band which played in the corner of the room.

Lottie looked around for a staircase and found one which led to an upper floor. At a table close to it sat a young woman who matched Barty's description. Anna Kofler was pretty, with blonde hair and large blue eyes. She looked about the same age as Lottie and was glancing about as if expecting someone to join her. Her hands rested on the table, fidgeting with a small, sequinned purse.

Lottie took another breath to bolster her confidence, then walked over and sat in the empty chair which Anna had presumably reserved for Barty.

'Anna?'

'Yes?'

'Teddy sent me here.'

Anna's face fell. 'He can't make it?'

'I'm afraid he can't.'

'You're his sister?'

'Sort of... actually, I'm not. My name is Lottie, and I used to work as a maid for Teddy's parents. I need to tell you a few things about him.'

Anna bit her lip. 'So he's not coming here this evening?'

'I'm afraid not. I think you deserve an explanation. I need to tell you he's not who he says he is. His name is Barty.'

'Not Teddy?'

'No. Barty.'

'So why did he lie?'

'Because he's a scoundrel. And that's his word, not mine. I'm afraid he likes to be friendly with ladies with no thought about what he's getting himself into. He's only just arrived here in Vienna. He was sent here by his family to join his aunt. I'm a travelling companion for his aunt.'

Anna's lower lip wobbled. 'I don't understand! Where's Teddy?'

Lottie realised she was doing a poor job of explaining everything. 'His name is Barty,' she repeated. 'Short for Bartholomew. And it's important that he stays out of your way now because you're going to be getting married soon and he doesn't want you to put an end to that.'

'He told you about that?'

'Yes, he did. You don't want to throw away what you have in the hope you can have a life with him. It wouldn't work, I'm afraid. Barty isn't a responsible person, and he acts before he thinks. He's frequently in trouble and seems unable to accept that any of it is ever his fault. He's very likeable and charming, as I'm sure you've discovered, but he only ever thinks about himself.'

Anna's face crumpled. 'But Teddy and I get on so well!'

'I'm sure you do. That's his nature. But Teddy isn't real. He's actually Barty, and he's got himself in trouble with his family and his university and now... with you. He gets himself in trouble with everyone. He can't help it.'

'Does he know you're here?'

'Yes. He asked me to meet you and explain everything.'

Anna scowled. 'So he's been lying to me? And he's too cowardly to meet me and admit it!'

This was the result Lottie had been hoping for. 'I'm afraid so.'

'He can't even show his face here and admit that he told me all those lies!'

'Yes.'

'What a...' Anna spat out a string of German words, and Lottie guessed they described Barty in unflattering terms. She nodded sympathetically and hoped Anna's plans to elope with him had now been abandoned.

Anna paused, then dabbed at her eyes. Then she gave a sniff, picked up her purse and got to her feet. 'I appreciate you being honest with me, Lottie. Although I don't know why you choose to associate with such a...' more German words followed.

'I merely work for his aunt,' said Lottie, once the torrent had stopped. 'I don't dislike Barty, but he has a lot of growing up to do.'

'He certainly has! When you next see him, tell him from me he has a Backpfeifengesicht.'

'Alright then. What does it mean?'

'It means he has a face that should be punched.'

'Alright then. I shall pass that on.'

'SHE SAYS I HAVE A *WHAT*?' said Barty when Lottie met him and Rosie in the park. Dusk was falling, and the birds were singing an evening song before they roosted in the trees.

'A backf... backfiff... sict, or something. Oh, I tried to remember it, but I can't now. Apparently, it means you have a face which should be punched.'

Barty grinned. 'It sounds like you did a good job of making her fall out of love with me!'

'Hopefully I did.'

'You weren't too horrible about me, though, were you?'

'No, I just told Anna the truth.'

'Alright. It must have been quite a hard-hitting truth if she said my face should be punched.'

'She didn't like being lied to, Barty. No one does. I told her your real name.'

'No!'

'There's no harm in it.'

'Yes, there is! I'm going to be in all sorts of trouble now!'

'Such as what?'

'Anything! There's a reason I call myself Teddy Farquhar. I

don't just do it for fun, you know. If people know my real name, then I end up suffering the repercussions of whichever scrape I've found myself in.'

'It wouldn't happen if you behaved yourself.'

'Oh, come on, Lottie, you sound like my mother and sisters.'

'But it's true.'

'I can't believe you told Anna my real name. Now she'll be onto me.'

'I didn't tell her your surname.'

'You didn't? Oh good. Thank you, Lottie. I mistakenly told her the name of the hotel we're staying at, but I can't imagine she's going to find me there and bother me, is she?'

'No, I don't think she has any interest in ever seeing you again.'

'She doesn't? Oh well, I suppose it's for the best. But I wish you'd kept up with the names we agreed.'

'I refuse to call myself Charity Farquhar.'

'It would only have been for ten minutes!'

'I don't like lying, Barty. I think it's much better the truth is out there. Everything has been cleared up and you won't be trying something like that again, will you?'

'No, although I didn't exactly do much in the first place. She fell in love with me!'

'Perhaps you'd be better off just staying in your hotel room for the rest of our time here. If you drag me into anything else like this while we're here in Vienna, then I shall tell your auntie! I've found it very difficult keeping this from her.'

'I won't get caught up in anything like this ever again, Lottie. You have my word.'

It was so difficult to believe that Lottie couldn't resist a smile.

Chapter Thirty-Four

MRS MOORE HAD a visitor after breakfast the following morning. 'Boris! Here you are again! You can't stay away from us, can you? Goodness. You don't look very happy. Is there bad news?'

'There is, I'm afraid.'

'Oh no. Is Prince Manfred alright?'

'Not really. He's rather shocked and upset.'

'He's been arrested again?'

'No. There's been another murder.'

'Another one? Who?'

'A waiter who has been working at Schönbrunn Palace this week. Can you believe it? A psychoanalyst and a waiter. Why would someone harm the pair of them?'

Lottie felt a chill run down her back. 'What's the waiter's name?' she asked.

'Anton.'

Mrs Moore's mouth hung open. 'Young Anton?'

'Yes, young. Very sad indeed. Did you know him?'

'No, not personally. But Lottie spoke to him just yesterday. He used to work for Dr Fischer, but the doctor sacked him and we wondered if he'd murdered the doctor out of revenge.'

Boris sighed. 'Well, that is interesting, I didn't realise Anton knew Dr Fischer.'

Lottie stroked Rosie as she tried to come to terms with this news. 'I don't understand it,' she said. 'Poor Anton.'

'When did this happen?' asked Mrs Moore.

'After dinner last night. And I'm afraid the attack was in the gardens again. Anton had left work for the evening and was making his way home when the killer attacked.'

'What did they do?'

'It appears he was struck on the back of the head with a heavy object. Much like Dr Fischer's murder. The police don't know what the heavy object is yet. They're searching the grounds for it.'

'So it wasn't a stone from the Roman ruin?'

'No. It must have been something the killer brought with them. Once again, the murder happened at dusk. There was a tall hedge close to the scene and the police think the killer must have lain in wait there. An ambush. It's completely terrifying! Who's next? I'm too afraid to stay at the palace now. I wish I could find a room at this hotel instead.'

'I'm not surprised,' said Mrs Moore. 'I'd be worried too.'

'I feel guilty now about suspecting Anton,' said Lottie.

'You discovered he had a motive, so you were quite right to suspect him,' said Mrs Moore. 'You weren't to know he'd become a victim himself, were you?'

'No.' Lottie felt sorry for the young waiter. Although she'd discovered he had a motive for murdering Dr Fischer, she'd found the young man likeable. She imagined Josef would be upset about it, too.

'Who was at the palace yesterday evening?' Mrs Moore asked Boris. 'Was the prince entertaining again?'

'No, he hasn't entertained there since the death of Dr Fischer.'

'So there was just you, Prince Manfred, and the palace staff?'

'Yes.'

'No other visitors?'

'None. And Prince Manfred didn't hear or see anyone when he went out for his evening stroll.'

'In the gardens?'

'Yes. He's been walking in the gardens every evening, watching the sunset. It's warm and pleasant and he's enjoyed being alone with his thoughts.'

'On his own?'

'Yes. Which is quite unusual for the prince because he usually likes company. He's certainly become a little quieter and withdrawn since Dr Fischer's death. I think he was quite upset about his arrest and although he knows the detective believes him, it has bothered him. He's never been in trouble with the police before.'

'Was Prince Manfred in the garden at the time poor Anton was murdered?'

'Yes, I believe he was. He says he didn't see or hear anything, though. Oh come now, Mrs Moore, I'm not sure I like that suspicious look on your face! Prince Manfred would have had absolutely nothing to do with Anton's murder.'

'But don't you think it's odd that he appears to have been close by when both murders were committed?'

'It's not odd, no. I think it's a coincidence, but nothing more than that. And besides, you'd expect him to be around because he's rented the palace for the week.'

'I'm sure Detective Inspector Berger will be interested when he discovers Prince Manfred's whereabouts at the time of Anton's murder,' said Mrs Moore.

'Yes, he will be. In fact, he's probably meeting with the

prince as we speak. No doubt I shall have to talk to him too, when I return to the palace. The prince is innocent, Mrs Moore. I really don't know what else I can do to persuade you of that fact. And besides, what reason could he have for murdering a waiter?'

'There may be some connection between them which we haven't discovered yet. After all, it was a surprise to find out Dr Fischer and Anton knew each other. It was also a surprise to discover Countess von Friedensberg and Dr Fischer knew each other.'

'They knew each other? I thought she met him for the first time on that evening?'

'No. Apparently, she was one of his patients.'

'Really?' Boris sighed. 'I never knew that. This is getting more and more complicated.'

'I'm going to visit Josef again,' said Lottie. 'He must know something.'

## Chapter Thirty-Five

THE GUARDS at the gate of Schönbrunn Palace recognised Lottie and Rosie, so they were admitted without a problem. Rosie managed to find Josef in the rose garden again, but his mood was solemn.

'Everyone's extremely upset,' he said. 'I liked Anton. I didn't know him very well, but he was friendly.'

'I liked him too,' said Lottie. 'It's difficult to believe this has happened.'

'He was walking home through the grounds after work,' said Josef. 'Just like he did every evening this week.'

Lottie wondered if the killer had known about this regular routine.

'He was found near the obelisk fountain by one of the gardeners at first light,' said Josef. He gave a shudder. 'I'm just relieved I wasn't the one who found him.'

'And he'd been hit over the head, like Dr Fischer?'

'That's what I heard.'

'How awful. I wonder what weapon was used?'

Josef shrugged. 'Who knows?'

'Apparently Prince Manfred was taking an evening walk in the grounds at the time of Anton's death,' she said.

The gardener's eyes widened. 'Really? And the button from his jacket was found at the scene of Dr Fischer's murder. That must be more than just a coincidence.'

'That's what I think, too. Prince Manfred says the button came off his jacket during a scuffle with Dr Fischer, but he didn't murder him. But he's the only person who appears to have been close to the scene of both murders.'

'Who are the other suspects in the murder of Dr Fischer?'

'I don't know what Detective Inspector Berger thinks, but I suspect Mrs Fischer, Countess von Friedensberg and Mr Smallwood. However, none of them were here yesterday.'

'That's right. From what I hear, Prince Manfred planned parties for each evening this week, but after Dr Fischer's death, he cancelled them. I haven't seen any guests here since then.'

'So that means the murderer could be a member of the palace staff.'

'But who?' said Josef.

'I don't know.'

'And why would they do such a thing?'

'It's impossible to know at the moment, isn't it? Another possibility is...' Lottie struggled to finish the rest of her sentence. She couldn't believe she was about to suggest such a thing. 'Boris. Prince Manfred's interpreter.'

'The small man in the blue suit?'

'Yes.'

'It can't be him! He's really friendly.'

'I know. It's tempting to believe the murderer is an obviously unpleasant person. But when you have to consider they could be someone you actually like... It's a difficult thing to consider.'

∾

Back at the hotel, Lottie had lunch with Mrs Moore and Barty. They sipped hot chicken soup from their spoons, and Lottie passed some pieces of bread to Rosie beneath the table.

'Did your gardener friend have anything helpful to say, Lottie?' asked Mrs Moore.

'Not much. But he confirmed there were no guests at the palace last night, just Prince Manfred and Boris.'

'So who attacked Anton the waiter?'

'I don't know. But Boris told us Prince Manfred was going for a walk in the grounds when Anton was attacked.'

'So he's the culprit after all? I still struggle to believe it.'

'So do I,' said Lottie. 'But I'm wondering if we've been foolish to believe everything Boris has told us.'

'What do you mean?'

'Prince Manfred and Boris are the only two people who were present near the scene of both murders. And I think we've made the mistake of believing everything Boris has told us. We've done so because we like him and trust him.'

'Yes we do, Lottie! He can't be a murderer and neither can the prince.'

'So how do you explain their innocence when they were close to the scenes of both murders?'

'Perhaps the two murders were committed by two different people.'

'Possibly. But there are a lot of similarities between the two attacks. Both took place in the evening in the grounds of the palace and both victims were hit over the head by something heavy.'

'Well, perhaps the second person is copying the first.'

'Perhaps they are. But it's still difficult to believe the prince and Boris had nothing to do with either death. The only other possible culprits would be a member of the palace staff.'

'There you go, then. That's your answer.'

Lottie shook her head. 'It doesn't seem right. And although Prince Manfred had an explanation for the button from his jacket being at the scene of Dr Fischer's death, it doesn't mean he didn't murder him during their scuffle.'

'You're right. It doesn't. Perhaps, from now on, we trust no one? I feel bad saying such things about Boris, but if he knows more about those murders than he's letting on, then it's quite right we should consider him. I don't believe Boris is a murderer though, I still refuse to think that. But as for Prince Manfred... the more I've learned about him in recent days, the less I like him. Oh, what's going on here?'

Mrs Moore picked up her lorgnette and trained them on a large, wide man with a thick grey moustache who was striding across the restaurant towards them. A waiter trailed in his wake, attempting to stop the man.

He stopped at their table and pointed a fat finger at Barty before saying something in German.

Barty gave a nervous smile then added, 'Good afternoon, sir! How are you?'

The waiter arrived at their table. 'I apologise,' he said. 'I told this gentleman not to disturb you, but he insisted on speaking to you, sir.'

'Me?' said Barty.

'Yes. He asked for you at the reception desk and the receptionist said he had seen you go into the restaurant for lunch.'

'How helpful of the receptionist. Who is this gentleman?'

'Herr Kofler.'

# Chapter Thirty-Six

THE SURNAME KOFLER was familiar to Lottie. It was Anna's surname. And the angry man now standing at their table was probably her father.

Barty appeared to have realised this too. He remained motionless, with an awkward grin fixed on his face. Herr Kofler was twice his size. The man's face was red and his enormous fists were clenched.

He barked something at Barty and pointed beyond the window. The waiter responded with something to placate him.

'What's happening?' asked Mrs Moore.

'Herr Kofler is asking Mr Barty to step outside for a fight,' explained the waiter.

'Oh no! Tell him we won't hear of such a thing!'

Lottie noticed Barty trembling a little. She understood now why he'd given Anna a false name. If Lottie hadn't told Anna his real name, then Herr Kofler wouldn't be here now.

Herr Kofler began shouting, and everyone in the restaurant turned to watch. Mouths dropped open and people muttered and pointed. The waiter gave up trying to placate him and left. Barty gave an uncomfortable laugh and pulled at his collar.

'Oh dear, Barty,' said Mrs Moore. 'What have you got up to? You told me you were avoiding scrapes.'

'I am! I've no idea why this hefty fellow has got a bee in his bonnet.'

'He clearly has a reason, Barty. I think you know more than you're letting on.'

'I can explain everything, Auntie, once he's calmed down.'

Herr Kofler's words eventually subsided. Then he raised a fist and uttered a few more.

'Have you quite finished?' Mrs Moore asked the gentleman. 'You're disturbing our lunch.'

Herr Kofler stepped back and nodded his head in apology. But then he pointed at Barty again and the diatribe continued.

Barty got to his feet.

'Don't go outside with him, Barty, whatever you do,' said Mrs Moore. 'He'll flatten you.'

'Don't worry, I have a plan.'

He found an empty chair at a neighbouring table and brought it over for Herr Kofler and gestured for him to sit.

'Drink?' he said. 'Shall we talk about this over a drink?'

Herr Kofler seemed to understand the word. He sat on the chair and glared at Barty.

'I won't be a moment,' said Barty. 'Back in a jiffy.'

Herr Kofler folded his arms and nodded at Mrs Moore again. Rosie ventured out from under the table and observed him. He looked at her but showed no further interest. Rosie retreated.

'Well, this is rather awkward, isn't it?' Mrs Moore said to Lottie.

'Very.'

Herr Kofler gave a sniff. Then he gestured at their bowls of soup. 'Please.'

'I think that means he's happy for us to keep eating,' said Mrs Moore. 'Let's do that. Not that we need his permission after he completely interrupted our pleasant lunch. Hopefully, Barty will be back in a moment to sort all this out.'

THEY ATE in silence for the next ten minutes. And as time passed, Lottie realised Barty wasn't returning.

Herr Kofler seemed to think the same. He kept glancing around and breathing heavily through his nose. Lottie was keen for him to leave.

Eventually, the large man grew restless. He asked Mrs Moore a question in German.

'I'm sorry, but I don't have the slightest idea what you're saying,' she replied. 'I don't know where my nephew's got to. It's obviously taking him a while to find the drinks.'

It was difficult to know if Herr Kofler understood this. He got to his feet, muttered something else, then managed a word in English, 'Goodbye.'

Mrs Moore shook her head in dismay as she watched him leave. 'Barty can't stay out of trouble for even a day, can he? Wait until I get my hands on that boy.'

## Chapter Thirty-Seven

'I SHOULD NEVER HAVE COME to Vienna. Everything has gone wrong!' Prince Manfred sat slumped in a chair in Catherine Fischer's dimly lit library.

Catherine felt little affection for him now. The jovial, happy prince she'd fallen in love with had gone. Instead, she was encumbered by a morose man feeling sorry for himself.

'I suppose we've been punished,' she said.

'Yes, we have! It's not fair. Everyone thinks I'm a murderer.'

'Not everyone. The detective released you without charge. And besides, people probably think I'm a murderer too.'

'No, they don't!'

'But they have very little sympathy for me, even though I'm now widowed. News of the affair between you and me makes Felix look like the wronged victim. If only everyone knew what he was like! They've got no idea what I endured when married to him. He was unfaithful throughout our marriage. And what did I do? I had just one love affair and everyone now thinks I'm a bad person. And probably a murderess, too.'

'I don't think that.'

'No. I know that.'

'Why don't you tell everyone what he was like?'

'Who would listen? They would think I was trying to make excuses for my behaviour. It never looks good to speak badly of the deceased. Once someone is dead, they can do no wrong. They become a good person. And anyone who was unkind to them is bad.'

'I don't think you're bad.'

'No, I realise that, Manfred, thank you.' She felt irritated by him. Couldn't he think of anything helpful to say at a time like this?

'Everyone thinks I'm bad,' he said.

'Boris doesn't.'

'Boris is the only friend I have left in this world. Even you don't love me anymore, Catherine.'

'I don't know how I feel about anything at the moment. It's a difficult time.'

'So you don't love me?'

'I didn't say that. I just don't know how I feel about anyone or anything right now. I'm struggling with grief.'

'So am I. Felix was my friend! I feel consumed by guilt. And the waiter too! I didn't know him, but he served me my meals and now he's dead! I've never felt this bad in my life before.'

'Have you got a good lawyer?'

'I don't know. I'll ask Boris.'

'I've got a good lawyer. It's very important at a time like this. You never know when the police are going to come for you.'

'They've done that already! Do you think they'll do it again?'

'Of course. Two murders in the grounds of the palace you're staying in. It doesn't look good, does it?'

'But I'm an innocent man!'

'Maybe. But you need to think about how you're going to prove it.'

# Chapter Thirty-Eight

PERCIVAL SMALLWOOD WOKE WITH A START. He wasn't supposed to have fallen asleep. What time was it? He didn't want to turn on the light to find out, it could disturb his landlady. He sat on his bed fully clothed and rubbed at the pain in his neck from where he'd fallen asleep with his head at an awkward angle.

His suitcase sat on the floor by his bed. All his clothes were packed inside it, and he was ready to go. But what was the time? He'd meant to stay awake until one o'clock.

It was still dark outside and, at this time of year, daybreak was at half past four.

As if answering his question, the clock chimed in the square. He held his breath as he listened. One. Two. Three.

Three o'clock. It was already later than he'd planned. He had to take his chance now. His landlady was an early riser, and he couldn't afford to leave it any later than this.

How could he have fallen asleep? He'd desperately tried to remain awake, repeating a musical refrain in his mind which he wasn't happy with. The plan had been to find a pattern which worked better, but instead he'd dozed off. How foolish!

His head felt heavy, keen for more sleep. But there was no time for that now. He had to make an escape.

He edged himself off the bed and gently rested his socked feet on the floor. He planned to put his shoes on once he was outside. In the darkness, he groped around for his shoes and despaired at how difficult it was to find them. He'd merely put them next to the bed the previous evening. Had they somehow walked off by themselves?

Eventually, he found them. The suitcase was easier to locate. He stood now, shoes in one hand and the case in the other. Ideally, the shoes would be in the case, but it was too full. He'd barely been able to close it.

He crept over to where he thought the door was. It was either a cloudy or moonless night because there was hardly any light at all.

Where was the door?

He stubbed his toe on the leg of the washstand then froze in horror. He held his breath and clenched his teeth tightly as the pain from his toe shot up through his leg and into his belly. Why did a stubbed toe hurt so much? He panted a little, trying to distract himself from the pain. Now he felt light-headed. Was this a good idea?

The landlady slept in the room next to him. He felt sure she must have heard the toe stub. It had knocked the wash-stand against the wall. But fortunately, all remained silent.

Once the pain had receded, he moved to his left, to where he felt sure the door must be. Frustratingly, he had to lower his shoes to the floor to free up a hand to open the door. He turned the doorknob cautiously and paused when it gave a click. Had the landlady heard? He waited for a response from the room next door, but none came. Cautiously, he pulled open the door and felt disappointed to see how dark it was out on the landing.

He startled as the door knocked against his shoes which

he'd placed on the floor. How could he have been so foolish to leave them in the way? He ducked down to grab them and knocked his head on the edge of the door.

He stopped in his half-crouched position, teeth gritted and eyes screwed tight. This was it. He was going to be found out. His head throbbed where the door's edge had hit it. Why was he being so clumsy?

When no noise was forthcoming from the room next door, he breathed again. He found his shoes and carefully returned to a standing position. Then he stepped out onto the dark landing.

He decided to close the door behind him. That way, the landlady would merely assume he was in his room, still sleeping. This time he lowered his case rather than his shoes because it would be easier to locate the case in the darkness.

He closed the door as silently as possible and picked up the case again. He felt pleased with this achievement. All he had to do now was find the stairs. A thin rug covered the landing. He crept slowly in his socks and avoided the squeaky floorboard. He passed the landlady's bedroom without a hitch and then cautiously extended a leg in front of him, feeling for the rug with his foot. Within the next few yards, he would reach the staircase and he had to make sure he didn't miss the first step.

On he went, carefully extending each foot forward before he committed to the stride. It wasn't easy with a heavy suitcase weighing his body down on one side.

It was exhausting and he could feel his breath labouring with the concentration. His right arm ached from the suitcase. He wanted to move it to his left hand, but doing so risked making extra noise. He had to remain focused on what he was doing. He was making excellent progress.

Eventually, his socked foot felt the edge of the rug where it ended just before the stairs. He positioned himself at the top of the staircase and gave a sigh of relief. He was almost there. Before him were twelve stairs, and they led down to the small hallway and front door. The front door key was always in the lock, and he knew it turned easily, with no noise.

All he had to do was walk down the stairs, and he would almost be there. He told himself not to rush. The landlady was sound asleep. Another hour would pass yet before she got up.

The staircase was in complete darkness, and he didn't have a hand free to hold on to the handrail. But as long as he moved slowly and carefully, he felt sure he'd be alright.

Just one step at a time.

He manoeuvred down onto the first step and congratulated himself with a deep, controlled breath. One done, only eleven left to go.

Down he went to the second step. He couldn't see a thing, but that was alright because he was doing a brilliant job of navigating his way through the darkness.

Ten steps left.

He stepped down again, and the stair gave a creak. He paused but felt reasonably confident the landlady hadn't heard it. She'd not been woken by the other noises he'd made, so he couldn't imagine the slight creak would cause any problems.

And he was proved correct. No sound came from the landlady's room.

He stepped down again. Nearly there.

But his suitcase collided noisily with the bannisters. He'd assumed he was in the centre of the step! How had he veered over to his right?

He corrected himself, but a little too much. The suitcase swung into his legs. What had made it so heavy? He stumbled and tried to find his balance, but it was impossible with a heavy case. Suddenly it was completely in his way and he was tipping forward.

Surely he could stop himself? But he couldn't.

He tumbled over the case, completely disorientated by the darkness.

The breath was knocked from him as he rolled and bounced down the remaining stairs. His suitcase and shoes came tumbling after him.

*Chapter Thirty-Nine*

'WHERE'S MRS MOORE THIS MORNING?' asked Lottie as she and Barty had breakfast.

'I think I may have brought on one of her headaches,' he said.

'Oh no.'

'I hid in my room for the rest of the day yesterday because I didn't fancy being flattened by Herr Kofler. But she knocked on my door in the evening and tore a strip off me.' He shook his head. 'Auntie can be pretty fearsome when she's riled.'

'What did she say?'

'There was a lot of talk about her being disappointed in me. There were a number of instructions too, such as the requirement to pull my socks up. She also said she plans to march me back home where I can receive a proper telling off from Father. However, having received tellings off from both of them I can honestly say that Auntie is the scarier one.'

'I can imagine.'

'I have to say I deserved it. I accept responsibility for the misunderstanding with Anna and I've assured Auntie it won't happen again. I knocked on her door this morning to apologise some more but she told me to go away because she's got one of her headaches.'

'Poor Mrs Moore.'

'I'll buy her a lovely bunch of flowers, that will help. And I'll make it up to her when she's feeling better. Meanwhile, what do you say to the carriage ride today?'

'I'd like to do that. How about this afternoon? I'd like to speak to a few people this morning.'

'What sort of people?'

'I want to find out what happened to poor Anton the waiter.'

'Oh, leave all that to the police, Lottie.'

'I'm sure they're working hard on it. But I feel like I've done a lot of work on it too. And if we're returning to England soon then I want to find out who did it.'

Barty gave a sigh. 'Good luck with that, Lottie.'

## Chapter Forty

'I REALLY DON'T KNOW what's happening at that palace,' said Catherine Fischer. 'Manfred needs to move out of there immediately, and it needs to be shuttered up. A madman is roaming the grounds!'

'If there is, then why hasn't anyone seen him?' asked Lottie. She sat in Mrs Fischer's dingy library with Rosie on her lap. Rosie was keen to say hello to a cat sitting by the fireplace, so Lottie kept a firm hand on her collar.

'How do you know no one's seen the madman?' Mrs Fischer asked her.

'I know one of the gardeners, Josef, and he would have said if he or his colleagues had seen a madman wandering around the gardens. Or anyone who looked suspicious, for that matter.'

'Poor Anton. If only my husband hadn't been so mean to him.'

'When we last spoke, you denied knowing him.'

'Did I? How strange of me. I was consumed with grief at the time. I probably wasn't thinking straight. I must admit it was only after I heard about Anton's murder that I recalled he knew my husband.'

'And he knew you as well.'

'Yes, but I didn't agree with how Felix treated him. There was no need for my husband to tell all his friends and patients not to employ Anton. What a horrible thing to do! When I found out what my husband had said about Anton, I told him off. But by then, it was too late. The damage had been done. Awful, isn't it?'

'I spoke to Anton about his refusal to serve your husband at dinner. He hadn't been expecting you both at the dinner that evening.'

'That makes sense. It was a rather last-minute decision of ours to attend and I can imagine he was surprised. He was probably hoping he'd never see my husband again after the way he treated him. And then he was expected to wait on him!'

'For a short while, I wondered if Anton was your husband's murderer.'

'Goodness, did you? You thought Anton could have been so upset that he actually murdered Felix?'

'I wasn't sure. I didn't know Anton very well, but he seemed pleasant so I couldn't imagine him being capable of such a thing. But there was no doubt he resented Dr Fischer and perhaps the pair of them bumped into each other in the palace grounds and argued before the murder.'

'Well, there's a thought.'

'But now Anton has fallen victim to the same attacker, I realise he wouldn't have done such a thing,' said Lottie. 'I feel guilty for suspecting him.'

'I wouldn't feel guilty. After all, the finger is being pointed at just about everyone, isn't it? With very little evidence, there are going to be a good number of suspects. I suppose the question is now, who murdered Anton?'

'Yes. As well as your husband.'

'A madman, I tell you. Only a madman is capable of such a thing. And I know the staff at the palace haven't seen one wandering about the place and that's because the madman is very clever.'

'Really?'

'Yes. The madman can disguise himself as a normal person who blends in with the rest of us. He's able to go about his daily business pretending to be completely and utterly normal. And then, all of a sudden... he kills! He's a monster in disguise. Shocking, isn't it?'

Lottie nodded in agreement.

'And the problem with such madmen is they're incredibly difficult to spot. They've probably spent their entire life being perfectly nice when they want to be, and very few people will ever have any idea what they're truly capable of. It worries me, it really does!'

Mrs Fischer's words were disconcerting. And as she described someone who disguised their evil so well, Lottie couldn't help thinking about Prince Manfred again.

Chapter Forty-One

PERCIVAL SMALLWOOD LAY on his bed, staring at the ceiling. His suitcase and shoes sat on the floor next to the bed. A dull pain throbbed in his lower back, growing sharper occasionally and making him wince.

He groaned with shame as the memory of being discovered at the foot of the stairs returned to him. The hallway light had been blinding and the expression on the landlady's face had been furious. But he'd also noticed a slight smile play on her lips as she realised he hadn't got away as he'd intended.

He felt now the part of his left wrist where his watch had once been. It felt strangely bare and incomplete.

Even as he'd lain crumpled with pain at the foot of the stairs, his landlady had reminded him he owed her a week's rent. He'd originally told her he would pay it after his performance. But Prince Manfred had never paid him! It was all the prince's fault!

These rich men were all the same. They expected everyone to do things for them as a favour.

He let out a cry as he felt another painful muscle spasm in his back. This was debilitating! He had no money because of

Prince Manfred, and he didn't know when he'd next be able to sit at a piano again. It was disastrous.

He wasn't proud of how he'd attempted to leave the lodging house without paying. He'd tried to explain his predicament to his landlady, but as neither spoke each other's language, it had been difficult. She hadn't understood that Prince Manfred had refused to pay him. She just thought he was a criminal. Especially now she had caught him trying to escape.

Now she had his watch, and it was a very good watch which would fetch a lot of money if it were sold. Through an exchange of broken English and broken German, they'd agreed that he had five days to find the money he owed her. If he didn't manage it, then she could sell his watch.

He didn't want to lose his watch. It had belonged to his father. If only Prince Manfred could pay him the five hundred krone he'd asked for, then all his problems would be solved.

But now he was broke and stuck. Lying on a bed, unable to pay his rent or play the piano.

## Chapter Forty-Two

'Oh, it's you,' said Countess von Friedensberg when Lottie and Rosie stepped into her cluttered salon. 'Where's your employer?'

'She's not very well this morning.'

'Oh dear, how sad. Do pass on my regards. Grape?'

'No, thank you.'

'And does your lovely doggy feel like saying hello? Here doggy, doggy!'

Rosie retreated behind Lottie's legs.

'She's feeling shy,' said Lottie.

'Clearly,' replied the countess, popping a grape into her mouth.

'I didn't realise you knew Dr Fischer,' said Lottie.

'I knew him?'

'That's what his wife, Catherine, told me. She said you were a patient of his.'

'Oh.'

'And yet you told everyone you didn't know him.'

The countess sighed. 'Because I was a patient of his. Who wants to admit that? And after he died, I denied I knew him because I felt sure everyone would accuse me of murdering him.'

'Why would they do that?'

'Because that's what people do. I decided it was safer to pretend I had nothing to do with the man. Is there anything else?'

'Did you know Anton, the waiter who was murdered in the grounds of the palace the other evening?'

'Awfully sad! I didn't know him at all, I'm afraid. Now you must excuse me, I'm expecting another visitor.'

The countess clearly wanted Lottie to leave and there was little she could do about it. 'Of course. Thank you for your time, Countess.'

As LOTTIE and Rosie left the house, a young, pretty woman with blonde bobbed hair was climbing the steps to the door. She wore a jade green low-waisted dress and carried a leather satchel.

Lottie stopped on the steps. 'Anna?'

The young woman paused, then scowled. Lottie realised she associated her with Barty and therefore didn't like her very much. 'It's a surprise to see you here,' said Lottie. 'Do you know the countess?'

'Yes, I do.'

'What a funny coincidence.'

'I'm guessing you know her as well.'

'A little. We were both present on the night Dr Fischer was murdered.'

Anna's eyes widened. 'You were there too?'

'Yes. My employer was invited to the palace by Prince Manfred and I accompanied her there.'

'Do you think Prince Manfred did it?'

'I don't know. It's a difficult case to solve.'

'It's like the plot of a detective novel,' said Anna.

'Do you like reading those? I love detective novels,' said Lottie.

'You do? I suppose we have something in common then. I would love to write a detective novel.'

'Then you should!'

'I will, one day. At the moment, I don't have much time. I'm busy writing romance novels.' She patted the bulky satchel.

'You've got one of your manuscripts with you now?'

'Yes. There's still a bit of work to do on it yet.'

'I can see now why you're visiting the countess. Presumably she's been offering you some writing advice?'

Anna gave a wry smile. 'Something like that.' Then she lowered her voice. 'Although, between you and me, I'm actually the one helping her. One day I'll write a book which has my own name on the cover.'

## Chapter Forty-Three

LOTTIE REFLECTED on her conversations with Mrs Fischer and Countess von Friedensberg as she walked with Rosie and Barty across the sunny Maria-Theresien-Platz. It was a large square bordered on two sides by elegant museum buildings. In the centre of the square stood a large monument with a throned queen at the top.

Catherine Fischer still seemed keen on the idea of a madman, but was she really referring to Prince Manfred? And although the countess had now admitted to knowing Dr Fischer, she was still tight-lipped about him. Lottie felt sure both women were hiding something. How could she discover what it was?

'There's our wagon!' said Barty, pointing to a shiny, open-topped carriage. Two grey horses stood between the shafts. The coachman wore a bowler hat and a long dark coat. He greeted them and gestured for them to climb on board. Barty helped Lottie into the carriage and she made herself comfortable on the leather seat.

'Isn't this exciting?' she said to Rosie. She lifted the corgi and placed her on the seat next to her.

189

'Take us for a spin please, coachman!' said Barty.

The horses began to move, and Lottie enjoyed the clop of their hooves on the ground.

'Forget motor cars,' said Barty. 'This is the way to travel.'

They left the square and trotted onto the tree-lined ring road. Lottie felt the warm breeze on her face.

'I bumped into Anna Kofler earlier,' she said to Barty.

'Oh dear. How is she? Not too broken-hearted, I hope?'

'No, she seems fine.'

'Excellent.'

'I didn't realise she was a writer.'

'Yes, she told me all about it, but I can't say I took it all in because books don't interest me very much. I remember her telling me she writes books for a rich woman who pretends she's the author. Seems a bit of a swindle to me.'

'Countess Marie von Friedensberg?' said Lottie.

'Who? I don't know. She didn't tell me her name.'

'I saw Anna at the countess's home and she told me she helps the countess with her writing. I think it probably means she writes the books for her. What a scandal!'

'I believe the countess pays her for it.'

'Do you know how much?'

'Fifty krone, I think.'

'Is that all? That's about the cost of a meal for two people in a restaurant. And yet the countess is apparently one of the bestselling authors in Austria!'

'And she pays Anna only fifty krone a book? Tell me where she lives! I'm going to go round there and give her a piece of my mind!'

'No, that's not a good idea, Barty.'

'Not a good idea? Why not? I know I can be a bit of a scoundrel myself at times, but I can't bear people who take advantage of others!'

'I'll make sure we ask the countess about it, Barty. She

doesn't know we have this information and there may be more we can gather about her. It's much better to put such things to her at a planned time.'

'Genius! You're a clever lass, Lottie.'

'I don't know about that.'

'So when you saw Anna, did she—woah!'

The carriage gave a lurch. The coachman cried out and slumped over in his seat. The reins loosened, and the horses took off.

Lottie gripped the side of the carriage. 'What's happening?' she cried out.

'He's collapsed!'

The horses cantered off down the road, veering around vehicles and scattering everyone in their path.

'I need to get hold of the horses!' said Barty. He lunged forward and tried to grab the reins which had slipped from the coachman's hand. 'It's no use, he's in the way! We need to haul him up!'

He grabbed the coachman under the arms and pulled him into a sitting position. The coachman's head lolled, and his hat fell off.

Panic gripped Lottie. Was the coachman dead?

'I need you to hold him upright, Lottie!' said Barty over his shoulder. 'Then I can fit on the seat next to him!'

The horses continued to canter as Lottie put her arms over the back of the seat and gripped the coachman's coat so she could hold him in position. It wasn't easy as the carriage rocked and the coachman's limp body was heavy. He pitched about with the movement of the carriage as she tried to keep hold of him.

Barty climbed over the back of the seat and sat himself next to the unresponsive coachman.

'You can rest him against my shoulder, Lottie! But hang onto him, still!'

The carriage lurched from side to side as the horses dashed along the street. Lottie caught flashes of people watching open mouthed. A man tentatively stepped forward to catch the horses' reins but thought better of it as they charged past.

'Woah!' Barty called out to the horses. He had hold of the reins now, but the horses weren't stopping.

Lottie's mouth was dry. She felt sure the carriage was going to topple over. As she remained stuck in her position, holding up the coachman, she couldn't turn her head to see how Rosie was faring. She could only hope the little dog was staying put and not trying to leave the carriage out of fright.

They rounded a corner into a market.

'Mind out of the way!' Barty called out to the people in front of them.

Lottie's arms ached as she clung onto the coachman. All she could do now was put her trust in the horses as Barty battled to control them. The gap between the market stalls was too narrow for the carriage to pass through, but the horses continued anyway. Lottie screwed her eyes shut and prayed it would all end quickly and safely.

The carriage hit a stall on the right, and she heard shouts and the splintering of wood. The impact sent the carriage leaning to the left, where it jolted as it hit another stall. She heard clattering as tables and crates fell to the floor. The carriage bumped up and down as its wheels travelled over debris.

The horses moved faster, startled by the noise they were causing.

'Woah!' Barty called out again. Lottie opened her eyes to see he had a firm grip on the reins now, but this wasn't enough to slow the horses. Once they were through the market, Barty steered them into a wider street. Finally, the horses broke their canter and slowed to a trot, but they tossed their heads restlessly.

'Calm down!' Barty shouted to them. Then he said over his shoulder, 'I suppose these horses only know German and I can't speak a word of it!'

Lottie noticed the coachman stirring. 'He's not dead!' she cried out, thoroughly relieved.

Although the coachman could hold his head up, he was still slumped against Barty and seemingly drowsy.

They entered a square with an enormous cathedral in the centre.

'Watch out!' shouted Barty to the people around them. Pedestrians leapt out of the way, and Barty appeared to have enough control on the reins now to steer the horses around the cathedral. Before long, they had completed a circuit and Barty set them on a course to repeat it. The trotting horses slowed.

'Hopefully they're getting bored now,' said Barty.

He tugged on the reins some more and the horses flung up their heads and pulled against him. Eventually, they gave in and slowed to a complete stop.

Lottie gave a laugh of relief. She let go of the coachman and left him slumped against Barty. She spun round and was relieved to see Rosie still on the seat, her tongue lolling out of her mouth as if nothing out of the ordinary had happened. Lottie gathered the dog up in her arms and gave her a hug.

The coachman groaned and rubbed the side of his head.

'Are you alright?' asked Barty.

He groaned and rubbed his head again. 'Katapult,' he said.

'Catapult?' replied Barty. 'Like one of these things?' He made a slingshot gesture with his hands while still holding the reins.

'Lottie, did you hear that?' said Barty, looking over his shoulder. 'Poor old coachman here is talking about a catapult. Someone must have fired it at the side of his head!'

'How awful! Why would someone do that?'

'I don't know. I didn't see anything. Did you?'

'No, nothing.'

The coachman turned to Barty and thanked him. Then he offered to take the reins.

'Ah wait, are you alright to drive?' Barty asked him. 'I think you need to see a doctor first.'

To their relief, another carriage pulled up alongside them. 'I'll look after him,' said the second coachman.

'He needs to see a doctor,' Barty explained. 'Someone's fired a catapult at him!'

## Chapter Forty-Four

AT DINNER, Lottie could feel herself still trembling from the carriage ride ordeal. Mrs Moore joined her and Barty, having recovered from her headache.

'What a thing to do,' said Mrs Moore. 'That poor coachman. Although I must say, Barty, it was extremely courageous of you to grab the reins as you did and get that carriage under control.'

'Thank you, Auntie. The horses still ran amok for a while, though.'

'They would have created even more chaos if you hadn't done what you did. Well done, Barty. I'm proud of you.'

'Really? Thank you, Auntie.'

'I wonder if the person who fired it was trying to aim at someone else,' said Lottie.

'Who?'

'Me!'

'You, Lottie?' said Barty. 'Why on earth would someone fire a catapult at you?'

'Because of the murder of Dr Fischer and the waiter! I've

been asking lots of questions and gathering information. What if the murderer wants to stop me?'

'By firing a catapult at you?'

'Yes!'

'But you saw what the projectile did to that enormous great coachman, Lottie. If it had hit your little head, then you would have been stone dead!'

'Exactly!' Lottie felt a shiver. 'Perhaps the murderer tried to kill me!'

'No,' said Barty. 'I refuse to believe it. No one could be that evil. I realise he or she has murdered two people, but to fire a catapult at you, Lottie? It would have to be a dreadfully evil person to do that. It was probably boys messing around. Perhaps they didn't intend to hit anyone but just wanted to startle the horses. I don't think you should consider such awful thoughts.'

'I agree,' said Mrs Moore. 'Don't start to worry you were the target, Lottie.'

'On the other hand,' said Barty, 'perhaps the catapult was meant to be aimed at me? Perhaps it was Herr Kofler? You saw how angry he was with me. Maybe he wants me dead.'

'There's little doubt Herr Kofler is an aggressive individual,' said Mrs Moore. 'But I can't imagine he would try to kill you, Barty. We may never know the answer. But I do know that it's yet another unpleasant incident in what has turned out to be a disastrous visit to Vienna. I wish we'd never come! I shall make plans for our return to England first thing in the morning.'

'But what about solving the murders of Dr Fischer and Anton?' asked Lottie.

'I know you're reluctant to leave it unresolved, Lottie. But what more can we do? It's probably most likely that Prince Manfred did it. I have no interest in defending him now.

Detective Inspector Berger seems quite competent, so let's leave it with him.'

'But I discovered a few more things today which I think he'll be interested to hear.'

'Very well. Why don't I send him a telegram and ask him to visit us here tomorrow morning? Then you can pass on what you've found out and leave him to do the rest.'

It wasn't the satisfactory resolution Lottie had hoped for. But she knew better than to argue with Mrs Moore once her mind was made up.

## Chapter Forty-Five

AFTER BREAKFAST THE FOLLOWING MORNING, Mrs Moore and Lottie were summoned to the reception desk.

'Detective Inspector Berger must be here,' said Mrs Moore. 'Hopefully it won't take long to tell him what you've found out, then we can get our railway tickets booked.'

The receptionist directed them to the lounge, where their visitor awaited.

But it wasn't the detective. Instead, the composer, Percival Smallwood, sat in a chair looking pale, thin and uncomfortable.

'Goodness, Percy,' said Mrs Moore as she and Lottie sat down. 'Are you alright?'

'No, I'm not.'

'What's happened?'

'I had an accident.'

'What sort of accident?'

'I fell down a staircase, and it's all Prince Manfred's fault.'

'Golly! He pushed you?'

'He may as well have done.'

'So he didn't push you?'

198

'No. But he refused to pay me for my performance, so I had no money for my lodgings. The landlady kept hassling me for payment, understandable on her part, I suppose. In the end, I was compelled to leave in the middle of the night, but it was so dark, I couldn't see the staircase.'

'Oh no! And you fell down it?'

'Yes. So I'm penniless and in constant pain in my back. All because that prince wouldn't pay me!'

'The more I hear about him, the more I dislike him.'

'You're friendly with Boris, aren't you?'

'Yes.'

'Could you ask Boris to arrange for my payment? I tried speaking to him about it, but it was in the presence of the prince and he kept making excuses for why he couldn't sort it out. I don't know where else to turn and I really would like my father's watch back.'

'What's happened to your father's watch?'

'The landlady has it and she's going to sell it in a few days if I can't raise the money.'

'Oh Percy! How awful for you!'

'It is. Usually when I'm having a difficult time, I play the piano to cheer myself up. But I'm in so much pain, I can't.'

'Oh Percy, it's a terrible predicament!'

'It truly is. Do you think you can help? I really don't know what else to do. I need the watch back from my landlady.'

'I'll speak to Boris for you, Percy, but I can't promise my words will do anything. Even if Boris agrees you should be paid, it's probably quite difficult for him to persuade the prince to pay. And to think he's forked out all that money to rent the palace for a week! And yet he can't even pay a performer.'

'I know. I wish I'd never met him now. And to think I was so excited to be invited to Vienna again! All that's happened is I've been caught up in a horrible murder case and I've lost all my money and I have back pain so severe that I don't know when I'll play the piano again.'

'Oh, you poor soul, Percy. Look, I have some money, why don't I lend you some?'

'No, I won't hear of it. It needs to come from the prince. He owes me money and, when he pays it, my finances will be in order.'

'But won't you at least allow me to—'

He held up his hand. 'No, I refuse all your offers of charity, Mrs Moore. Even though I'm extremely grateful to you for making them. This is the prince's responsibility and all I ask is you have a word with him on my behalf. Perhaps he'll take pity on me.'

'He should, you're in an absolute state!'

'I should never have come here. I should have learnt to stay away from Vienna after my last visit when Dr Fischer didn't pay me either. These chaps are all the same!' He said this with a raised voice, then winced. 'Ouch. That hurt my ribs.'

'Have you been checked out by a doctor?'

'Not yet.'

'Mrs Moore!'

They turned to see Boris and Prince Manfred entering the lounge.

Mrs Moore gave a loud groan. 'Oh no.'

The prince's appearance was out of character. He wore a dull grey suit and the dark curls on his head were limp.

'Prince Manfred begs himself to be remembered to you,' said Boris. The prince sank into a chair nearby while Boris stood awkwardly in front of Mrs Moore.

'Why?' she asked.

'He has fond memories of your time in Monaco together.'

'They certainly are fond memories. But a lot has happened since then.'

'The prince wishes to assure you he had nothing to do

with the murders of Dr Fischer and Anton, the waiter. He's been terribly upset by the dreadful incidents.'

'I don't think it's me he needs to persuade, Boris, it's Detective Inspector Berger.'

'Ah, but he realises you once held affection for him and he would very much like—'

'That was before I found out he was having a love affair with Mrs Fischer.'

'The prince is capable of holding more than one person in his heart.'

'Is he? How charitable of him. I, however, don't like the idea of sharing him with other people. I believed, for a time, Boris, that the prince and I had a future together. However, I've now realised that we don't. And even if he had nothing to do with Mrs Fischer - or any other lady - again, my feelings on the matter won't change. And I've now learned he refused to pay poor Percival Smallwood for his delightful performance the other evening. I'm afraid my opinion of the prince has sunk even lower. I know you're a good friend of his and feel extremely loyal to him, so I apologise if you find my words upsetting. But the prince can do little now to redeem himself other than pay Mr Smallwood here the money he's owed.'

Boris nodded. 'Between you and me, Mrs Moore, the prince has difficulty paying people for their services.'

'Well, that's a difficulty he'll have to overcome. And it's a character trait I find most unappealing. Do you realise poor Mr Smallwood has had his father's watch confiscated from him and his back is so injured he doesn't know when he'll sit at a piano again?'

'No. Really?'

'And it's all the prince's fault because he refused to pay him.'

'I shall have a strong word with him, Mrs Moore.'

'It needs to be an extremely strong word, Boris. And if he

doesn't listen to you, then I advise you to cut all ties with him. I realise he's a lifelong friend, but that doesn't mean he's a nice person.'

'Manfred!' The shrill voice came from Catherine Fischer, who'd just swept into the lounge, dressed head-to-toe in a fashionable black mourning dress.

Mrs Moore gasped. 'Mrs Fischer? What are you doing here?'

'I've been trying to find Prince Manfred. He's been ignoring me, and I've been looking all over for him. Then I heard word that he'd come to this hotel, and I've found him here with you!'

'Yes. You're welcome to him.'

'Are you trying to snatch him away from me?'

'No. He's all yours.'

Lottie felt relieved to see grey-whiskered Detective Inspector Berger enter the room. Mrs Moore also seemed pleased to see him as she surveyed him through her lorgnette. 'Thank goodness you're here, Detective. It's getting a little confrontational here. Perhaps you can calm the troubled waters?'

'I shall do my best. I've asked Countess von Friedensberg to join us, too. She visited me this morning wishing to explain something. I told her I was coming to this hotel.'

'Before she arrives, my companion, Lottie, can tell you what she's found out over the past few days.'

'Of course.' He turned to Lottie. 'What do you wish to tell me?'

'I discovered Anton used to work for Dr and Mrs Fischer,' said Lottie. 'But Dr Fischer falsely accused Anton of stealing and spread the word throughout Vienna that he shouldn't be employed. When I first mentioned Anton to Mrs Fischer, she denied knowing him. But then she admitted she did after all.'

'I was caught up in my grief when she asked me the first time!' protested Mrs Fischer.

'And I spoke to Countess von Friedensberg,' continued Lottie. 'And she told me... well, here she is now. And perhaps she's ready to tell you what she told me.'

The red-haired countess walked into the room, looking sombre in a fashionable honey brown jacket and skirt.

Rosie nuzzled against Lottie's legs, clearly bothered by the appearance of the countess.

'Here we are, Countess,' said Detective Inspector Berger. 'What do you wish to tell us?'

## Chapter Forty-Six

'I KNOW one shouldn't speak ill of the dead,' said Countess von Friedensberg. 'But Dr Felix Fischer was a dishonourable man.'

'You were a patient of his, weren't you?' asked Mrs Moore.

'Yes, and I regret it.'

'Why?'

'Because he made me lie on that couch of his and tell him my deepest, darkest secrets! He retrieved them all from the recesses of my mind.'

'Isn't that what psychoanalysts do?'

'Yes. And usually you're able to trust them.'

'And what made you distrust him?'

The countess cleared her throat. 'It makes me uncomfortable talking about it, but I suppose I'd better give you all a proper explanation. He wanted to start a love affair with me.'

'No! How unprofessional of him!' said Mrs Moore.

'It doesn't surprise me in the slightest,' added Mrs Fischer.

'And I can tell you now, Catherine, that I wasn't the least bit interested in the idea. He would send a bouquet of flowers to my home every day, hoping such gestures would make me change my mind. They didn't, of course.'

'Why didn't you mention this sooner?' asked Mrs Moore.

'Because people might think I murdered him.'

'Just because you were a patient of his?'

'Yes.'

'That doesn't make sense,' said Detective Inspector Berger. 'No one would think you murdered Dr Fischer just because you'd been one of his patients.'

Lottie felt she had something useful to add. 'People might think Countess von Friedensberg murdered Dr Fischer if he'd threatened to reveal her secrets.'

The countess gave her a sullen look but said nothing.

'Such as what?' asked Mrs Fischer.

'Do you write your own books, Countess?' Lottie asked her.

'Of course!'

'You don't pay people a pittance to write them for you?'

'For as long as I've been an author, I have offered guidance to young people keen to make a living as an author. Sometimes they write pieces for me and I appraise them.'

'Do they write your books for you?'

'They contribute because it's a valuable experience for them. They're learning the skills to have a career as successful as mine.'

'I know someone who writes some of your books. Her name is Anna Kofler.'

'Never heard of her.'

'But you must have,' said Detective Inspector Berger. 'Why would Miss Sprigg invent a story like this?'

'I think she likes to create fiction too.'

'So we have a motive,' said the detective. 'During your sessions with Dr Fischer, you admitted you don't write your own books. He threatened to make this information public unless you had a love affair with him?'

The countess pursed her lips.

'So it's true?'

'You murdered him, Marie?' asked Mrs Fischer.

'I don't think Countess von Friedensberg murdered the psychoanalyst,' said Percy. 'I think it's quite obvious it's the prince! He was wicked enough to have an affair with his friend's wife, so I think he's wicked enough to murder the poor chap!'

'There's little doubt the prince has questionable morals,' said Mrs Moore. 'But there's quite a difference between deceit and murder.'

'I disagree,' said Mr Smallwood. 'I think Prince Manfred is a Jekyll and Hyde character. He pretends to be jolly and care-free, but it's a carefully constructed facade to hide the monster within.'

'Prince Manfred is a tactless, selfish fool,' said Boris. 'But there's not an ounce of evil in him.'

Lottie watched Prince Manfred listen to the conversation, clueless about what was being said. She imagined Boris wouldn't go to the trouble of translating his description of him.

'Well, can you explain why the prince's button was found at the scene of the crime?' said Mr Smallwood. 'If that's not damning evidence, then I don't know what is!'

'Prince Manfred has explained there was a scuffle between him and Dr Fischer,' said Boris. 'Dr Fischer apparently started it because he was understandably upset after discovering the affair between the prince and his wife. Prince Manfred says he had to defend himself.'

As Lottie listened to the discussion, she recalled the conversations she'd had with each of the people in the room. Most of them had tried to bend the truth in some way. But who had tried the hardest? And who'd been the least convincing? She had an idea now, and she hoped she was right.

'So, if the prince is not the murderer, who is it, Boris?' asked Percy.

The interpreter fidgeted with his hands. 'I don't know. But I'm tempted to say Mrs Fischer.'

'Me?' shrieked Catherine Fischer. 'I murdered my husband? Boris! How could you suggest such a thing?'

'I'm sorry, but what can I say? The marriage was unhappy, and you found love with the prince. It suited you both to have Dr Fischer removed.'

'I was planning to leave my husband,' said Mrs Fischer. 'I didn't need to murder him. I didn't like him anymore and his treatment of the countess is another example of how unpleasant he could be. Fancy threatening to reveal your patients' secrets! Awful behaviour. I realise my own actions were not perfect. Who can resist the charms of Prince Manfred of Bavaria? Europe's most eligible bachelor! I have to tell you now that I felt so lonely in my marriage to Felix. How wonderful it was to meet the prince and enjoy his sense of fun!'

Lottie noticed Mrs Moore give a sniff. Although she no longer held any affection for the prince, she'd once been fond of him and had imagined a fun-filled life with him.

Boris was whispering a translation to the prince. When he'd finished, Prince Manfred turned to Mrs Fischer and put his hand on his heart.

'The only person left to consider is Mr Smallwood,' said Lottie.

'Poor Percy,' said Mrs Moore. 'Here we are discussing the murder and he just needs paying for his performance!'

'I wouldn't feel so sorry for him, Mrs Moore,' said Lottie. 'I think Mr Smallwood is the murderer.'

## Chapter Forty-Seven

PERCIVAL SMALLWOOD BEGAN LAUGHING. 'Me? I've never heard anything so ridiculous in all my days!'

Mrs Moore turned to Lottie. 'Why are you accusing Percy?'

'Because, having listened to everyone's explanations, his is the one which makes the least sense.'

'How do you mean?'

'Do you remember when we encountered Percy after he'd supposedly found Dr Fischer's body? He was out of breath and his clothes were wet. Apparently because he'd just tried to save Dr Fischer, and he'd run across the gardens for help.'

'That's right,' said Percy.

'You told us you tried to save him,' said Lottie.

'Yes.'

'What did you do?'

'Obviously, I pulled him out of the water! And then I saw the head wound. I realised he must have slipped and hit his head and drowned!'

'You also told us you thought you saw two people at the

Roman ruin, but then thought it was just one. You said your eyesight wasn't very good.'

'That's right. My eyesight is terrible!'

'But you were wearing your spectacles.'

'I don't think I was.'

'You took them off for the recital but put them on again afterwards.'

'Did I?'

'And I remember you were wearing your spectacles when you told us you'd discovered Dr Fischer.'

'I don't recall.'

'So what did you see at the Roman ruin, Mr Smallwood?' asked Detective Inspector Berger. 'Two people or one?'

'Just one. I don't remember saying I saw two.'

Lottie turned to Detective Inspector Berger. 'When you first addressed us all that evening, you told us you'd found Dr Fischer dead in the pond at the Roman ruin.'

'That's right.'

'So he was still in the water?'

'Yes.'

'Even though Percy told us he'd tried to save him by pulling him out?'

The detective gave a nod. 'Very interesting, indeed, Miss Sprigg. He did say that, didn't he?'

'I *tried* to pull him out!' said Percy. 'But when I saw the head wound, I realised there was no point, so I dropped him again.'

'That's not what you said a minute ago,' said the detective. 'You said you pulled him out of the water. Why are you changing your story now?'

'I'm not!'

The detective turned back to Lottie. 'This accusation is clearly bothering Mr Smallwood. What other evidence do you have?'

'His recent behaviour. After Anton's murder, he tried to leave in the middle of the night.'

'Because I didn't have any money to pay my landlady!' said Percy.

'That's what you told us. But you could also have been trying to escape justice.'

'Nonsense.'

'I'm almost convinced, Miss Sprigg,' said the detective. 'But what motive did Percy have for murdering Dr Fischer?'

'Dr Fischer refused to pay him when he performed for him last year and it's clear he's still angry about it. When he left the music room after his recital, he was angry because most of his audience had either left or fallen asleep. He must have marched through that garden, desperate to confront someone about their rudeness. I think Dr Fischer had the misfortune of being the first person he came across. And when Percy saw him, his anger about not being paid no doubt resurfaced too. I think that by the time he confronted Dr Fischer at the Roman ruin, Percy was an extremely angry man.'

'Do you know the first thing he said to me?' said Percy. 'He told me my recital was boring! Can you imagine what it felt like to hear that? And when he refused to pay me last year he told me it was because he'd misunderstood our agreement. The discussion went on for a long time and he tried to patronise me with lots of long words. All meaningless and forming an extremely weak excuse for why he couldn't pay me. He assumed I was honoured to play for him! There was no honour in performing for that man at all. And I told him so when he insulted me at the Roman ruin!'

'Dr Fischer was probably in a foul mood after his tussle with Prince Manfred,' said the detective. 'With both gentlemen wound up like that, I can imagine it quickly got out of hand. So are you admitting to Dr Fischer's murder, Mr Smallwood?'

Percy sighed. 'As you've already said, detective, it got out of hand.'

'I'm not sure why Percy murdered Anton,' said Lottie. 'Anton told me he found Percy's performance amusing, but I don't know how that could have led to murder.'

'Because it wasn't supposed to be amusing!' snapped Percy. 'He was rude about me!'

'What did he do?' asked Lottie.

Percy took in a deep breath and exhaled. 'While Detective Inspector Berger was interviewing us all, I took a little stroll around the palace to calm myself. I passed the music room and heard the most awful din from beyond the door. I stepped in and saw that waiter, Anton, banging the keys and throwing his head about as if pretending to be me. His thick-headed friend was standing at the side of the piano laughing like a baboon. As soon as they saw me there, they were silent. But when I left the room, I heard them laugh uproariously again. No one makes fun of me like that and gets away with it.'

'So you murdered him?' asked the detective.

'Their laughter consumed me! It was a complete humiliation. I couldn't sleep from the shame! Having heard Anton had walked through the gardens on his way home on the evening of Dr Fischer's murder, I went back there to see if he used the same route each evening. As luck would have it, he did.'

'How did you get in?' asked Detective Berger.

'Quite easily. I just found a secluded section of wall and climbed over. And those foolish gardeners leave shovels lying around.'

'You hit him with a shovel?'

'I'm afraid so. He didn't know a thing.'

The room fell silent for a moment.

'If it helps at all...' said Percy. 'I didn't actually intend that anyone should die. I just wanted to teach them a lesson. But sometimes I don't know my own strength and... *that girl.*' Lottie startled as he pointed at her. 'I realised she was being nosy and I wanted to teach her a lesson too. When I saw her in that carriage I thought it would be great fun to startle the horses.'

'You fired the catapult at the coachman?' asked Mrs Moore.

'The stone was supposed to hit the carriage. I'm not a very good shot. There was a little boy nearby with a catapult and I borrowed it from him. When I saw the horses take off down the road, I couldn't help laughing! That's what you have to do at times like this, isn't it? Laugh!'

Lottie realised Mrs Fischer had been right all along. The murderer was a madman.

# Chapter Forty-Eight

'PERCIVAL SMALLWOOD MURDERED Dr Fischer because he hadn't paid him? Then murdered Anton because he laughed at him?'

Lottie nodded. 'Apparently so.'

Josef shook his head. 'He doesn't sound like the sort of person you want to fall out with.'

'No. It seems he has a fragile ego and a violent temper. A nasty combination.'

'Rolf was looking for his shovel yesterday and he couldn't find it anywhere. He always left his tools lying about, but he won't do it again.'

'I'm not surprised. But he couldn't have predicted a crazed composer would find his shovel and use it as a murder weapon.' Lottie sighed and glanced around the pretty rose garden. The warm sunshine brought out the heady scent of the blooms. 'I'm sorry two tragic events happened in these beautiful gardens you look after.'

'It's not your fault! I suppose if Prince Manfred ever hires this palace again, he'll have to think carefully about the guests he invites.'

'Thank you for all your help, Josef.'

They exchanged a smile. 'I don't think I did much to help, did I? Anyway, it was a pleasure.'

'I have to get back to the hotel. We're catching the train to Paris this afternoon.'

'And then back to England?'

'Yes. In fact, I'm looking forward to it. My travels with Mrs Moore have been quite an adventure.'

'I'm sorry you're leaving, Lottie. If you ever feel like writing to me, you know where to send the letter. Just address it to Josef Baumann at Schönbrunn Palace.'

Lottie laughed. 'That makes it sound like you own the place!'

'It does, doesn't it? It's fun to pretend occasionally.'

Lottie looked around for Rosie, then saw her sitting in Josef's wheelbarrow. 'I think Rosie wants a quick ride in the wheelbarrow before we leave.'

Josef chuckled. 'Oh, alright then. But just quickly. You don't want to miss your train.'

∽

When Lottie and Rosie arrived back at the hotel, Mrs Moore and Barty were waiting in the foyer with a sizeable pile of luggage. Lottie felt sure they'd acquired more cases on their travels.

'Oh, there you are, Lottie!' said her employer. 'I'm worrying we're going to miss the train!'

'We have two hours yet, Auntie,' said Barty. 'There really is no hurry at all.'

'Oh no...' Mrs Moore raised her lorgnette and peered through them at the hotel's entrance.

Lottie turned to see Boris and Prince Manfred walking towards them.

Once he reached them, Boris gave a polite bow. The prince stood behind him in a navy velvet suit. His expression was solemn.

'Prince Manfred begs your forgiveness,' Boris said to Mrs Moore. 'And he requests that you consider changing your mind about returning to England and travel with him to—'

'Not a chance!'

'Oh.'

'I'm sorry, Boris. I don't mean to snap at you. You have been a delightful companion during our travels and I wish you all the best for the future. Please inform the prince that my mind is made up about returning to England. I had some fun times with him and I shan't forget them, but I know when it's time to move on.'

'I see. The prince will be extremely saddened to hear this.'

'I'm sure he will. And I'm also sure he will be just fine. Goodbye Boris.'

'Goodbye Mrs Moore, it has been a pleasure knowing you.'

'We need to leave!' piped up Barty.

Mrs Moore turned to him. 'Leave? A moment ago you said there was no hurry at all.'

'There is now!'

Lottie caught sight of a large, wide man with a thick grey moustache striding towards them. 'It's your friend, Herr Kofler,' she said.

'Yikes! Can we go?'

'Yes, but we can't move quickly with all this luggage,' said Mrs Moore.

'I'll take mine.' Barty picked up a case. 'Then I'll ask the porters at the station to come here and collect the rest. See you there!'

Lottie giggled as she watched Barty's lanky frame dash across the foyer, side-stepping Herr Kofler as he went. The large gentleman gave a growl, turned and went after him. Lottie knew he had no hope of catching up.

'What a palaver,' said Mrs Moore. 'I'm looking forward to returning to England for a rest. How about you, Lottie?'

'I'm looking forward to it too.' She bent down and picked up her corgi. 'And I think Rosie will enjoy seeing her new home.'

Mrs Moore smiled and patted the dog on the head. 'She will indeed. Watch out Fortescue Manor, here we come!'

THE END

*Thank you*

Thank you for reading this Lottie Sprigg mystery. I really hope you enjoyed it! Here are a few ways to stay in touch:

- Join my mailing list and receive a FREE short story *Murder in Milan*: marthabond.com/murder-in-milan
- Like my brand new Facebook page: facebook.com/marthabondauthor

# *Murder in the Library*

**Book 1 in the Lottie Sprigg Country House Mystery Series.**

**Murder mystery at the manor!**

After months of travel, former maid, Lottie Sprigg, returns to Fortescue Manor in the rolling hills of Shropshire. Her arrival coincides with a celebratory dinner to mend a family feud. But the flow of champagne dwindles to a trickle when a body is found in the library...

Who committed the atrocity? Suspicion falls on several characters: some above stairs and some below. The local detective has his work cut out, and Lottie feels sure her sleuthing skills will help. With her trusty dog companion, Rosie, she embarks on the task.

But detective work can be dangerous. And when the killer strikes again, Lottie realises no corner of Fortescue Manor is safe.

Get your copy: mybook.to/murder-library

# A free Lottie Sprigg mystery

**Find out what happens when Lottie, Rosie and Mrs Moore catch the train to Paris in this free mystery *Murder in Milan*!**

Lottie and Mrs Moore are travelling from Venice to Paris when their journey is halted at Milan. A passenger has been poisoned and no one can resume their trip until the killer is caught. Trapped in a dismal hotel with her corgi sidekick, Lottie is handed a mysterious suitcase which could land her in trouble...

Events escalate with a second poisoning. Lottie must clear her name and find the killer before the trip is cancelled for good!

Visit my website to claim your free copy:
marthabond.com/murder-in-milan

Or scan the code on the following page:

# Also by Martha Bond

Lottie Sprigg Country House Mystery Series:

*Murder in the Library*
*Murder in the Grotto*
*Murder in the Maze*
*Murder in the Bay*

## Writing as Emily Organ:

Augusta Peel Mystery Series:

*Death in Soho*
*Murder in the Air*
*The Bloomsbury Murder*
*The Tower Bridge Murder*
*Death in Westminster*
*Murder on the Thames*
*The Baker Street Murders*

Penny Green Mystery Series:

*Limelight*
*The Rookery*
*The Maid's Secret*
*The Inventor*
*Curse of the Poppy*
*The Bermondsey Poisoner*
*An Unwelcome Guest*
*Death at the Workhouse*
*The Gang of St Bride's*
*Murder in Ratcliffe*
*The Egyptian Mystery*
*The Camden Spiritualist*

Churchill & Pemberley Mystery Series:

*Tragedy at Piddleton Hotel*
*Murder in Cold Mud*
*Puzzle in Poppleford Wood*
*Trouble in the Churchyard*
*Wheels of Peril*
*The Poisoned Peer*
*Fiasco at the Jam Factory*
*Disaster at the Christmas Dinner*
*Christmas Calamity at the Vicarage (novella)*

Printed in Great Britain
by Amazon

43243429R00131